MW01593828

A Dog's Choice

A Novel

"a shoplifter in the heart store"
Dona Schell, *Skating Through Coleman*

Allan Meyer

Arizona Vintage Investments, LLC   Oro Valley, Arizona

Copyright 2014 by Allan Meyer

All rights reserved. Except for brief quotations in reviews, no part of this book may be reproduced in any form without the written permission of the author.

A Dog's Choice is a work of fiction. All names and events are used fictitiously.

This edition was prepared for publication by
Ghost River Images
5350 East Fourth Street
Tucson, Arizona 85711
www.ghostriverimages.com

ISBN 978-0-9778701-2-7

LCCN 2013957050

Published in the United States of America
By Arizona Vintage Investments, LLC Oro Valley, AZ 85755
First Print Edition
January 2014

Contents

TO

Dogs everywhere, for permitting us to foolishly believe that we
are in charge

Dear Reader

A Dog's Choice is powered by a savvy dog that will neither sing nor roll over, by an aging cynic who cautions against obeying the Ten Commandments without first reading the fine print and by a four-year-old girl who distrusts Boston because "my dad says the place is full of Irishmen." They are part of a loveable disorder that once flourished in the fictional town of Hearts Landing, Arizona.

Ask The Snowplow Driver

Chapter 1

Sixty-six-year-old Eddie Grace paced nervously as he waited in the Tucson Airport for the puppy from far-away Big Icicle, South Dakota. When the flight left Denver 20 minutes late, he asked everyone about blizzards, unreported meteors and a possible hijacking. Not until a weary Christmas traveler assured him that the aircraft had not hit the control tower did Eddie actually get in line for the dog at the freight terminal.

As he wheeled the live animal kennel through the parking lot, he heard a feminine voice saying something about "grace" or maybe "grass;" he couldn't be sure. With no one near, he attributed the sound to either anxiety or to his chronic hearing problem. Then just for the fun of it, he looked directly at the puppy and asked, "Excuse me, did you just say something to me?" Without a wag or a whimper, the four-month-old puppy answered, "Get me out of this box, Cowboy, before Arizona gets another artificial lake."

Rattled, Eddie looked around again. Nothing. No gimmick card from JD on the crate, nobody who looked like a comedian. Standing motionless for thirty seconds, he thought, *this could be my introduction to Adult Protection Services.*

"You look pretty nervous right now," the puppy said. "What's wrong?"

7

"Wrong?" Eddie asked. "There are nearly seven billion people in the world and until today, no talking dogs. That's what's wrong." The puppy ignored the point.

"And moreover," Eddie said, "I'm a retired philosophy teacher and a natural target for bad jokes. Imagine a headline in tomorrow's paper, "Dog Talks to Philosopher–But Is She Real?"

"Okay, then we'll keep this matter private," the dog said. "I will talk only to you and not very often. At JD's place, I never talked out loud to anyone, unless you count that bark when his ex-wife sent the sheriff out to collect the overdue alimony. Now, doesn't that make you feel better?"

The correct answer was "no," because up to that point Eddie's life had been filled with sameness, not difference—same wife, same job (until retirement), same red wine every night at sundown. No sky-walking across the Grand Canyon, no four-vehicle collisions in a parking lot. In the high tech age, his only texting was a four-digit message to his garage door. Now how's a man like that going to deal with a dog that talks?

Despite his aversion to change and manufactured excitement, Eddie was not a loner or a misfit. His friends welcomed his company, his dean had repeatedly nominated him for professor of the year and in 40 years of marriage, Harriet hadn't said a word about wanting to trade up.

Just then a woman who had grudgingly dealt with two of his questions about air transportation safety a few minutes earlier walked briskly across the parking area. When she came within 10 feet, Eddie said, "Excuse me please, but do I look like I'm about to faint?" Smiling in disbelief, the woman said, "God, the poor dog," and kept moving.

After a second threat from the puppy, Eddie took her to a patch of grass for bladder relief.

"And don't 'good girl' me when I go or I'll pee on your shoes," the dog said.

"Pee on the governor, I don't care," Eddie said, "I just want to believe that the sky is still up there."

Picking up family or friends at the airport was always so simple, Eddie thought. *I acted happy, grabbed a suitcase and tried not to pull a muscle while reaching out the car window to pay the parking fee. Why couldn't JD have sent the musical rain gauge from Old Squirrel, Kentucky, instead of a talking dog?*

"Look, before you run back to your mother," the puppy said, "let me introduce myself. My name is Zelda, and I am a woman, canine–a throwback to the time when dogs talked. We can work out the rest as we go."

Afraid that someone might hear them "talking," Eddie quickly put the crate into the trunk of the Volvo and gave Zelda the front seat for the short ride to her new home in Hearts Landing. As he paid the parking charge, the attendant said, "Don't look so worried, man. In no time that little guy will be talking up a storm, just like a grandkid."

North of downtown Tucson, Eddie cautiously asked, "Aren't you a little frail?"

"Who are you calling frail, Cowboy? Bring on your rattlesnakes."

"You're already getting a little loud," Eddie said. "I don't like loud. You can be loud when there's a fire."

"After 1,300 miles, I'm hungry." Zelda said. "Could you speed up a little?"

"And I never drive fast. We have two of everything Purina makes. You'll be fat in three weeks."

With food in her future, Zelda announced, "Well then, it's all scttlcd. As thc only talking dog in existence, I would like a town named for me when I die. I am, after all, the first of my kind and therefore there can never be another, first, that is. I'm George Washington with four legs and a lot better looking coat."

Thirty minutes later, Eddie introduced Zelda to the backyard where she acted like the place was hers by birthright.

"Her coat is gorgeous and she's perky," Harriet said between hugs. "You look a little worn out, Dear, was the plane late?"

9

"Only a few minutes," Eddie said. "Getting out of the airport was slow."

"I hope she likes the pillows. They didn't have a lot of choices at Everything Hastings." Harriet had memorized the bedding inventory in every pet department in northwest Tucson.

Still as nervous as a rookie pitcher in Yankee Stadium, Eddie said, "I think if she doesn't like them she'll let us know."

The phone rang and both he and Harriet picked up.

"Hello," Eddie said.

"How do you like your new sweetheart?" JD asked.

"We like her, but why did you think she was so right for us?" Eddie asked, hoping for an answer to the big question.

"It's like this," JD said, "one cold night a month ago I hear a noise in the house. I grab a flashlight and see this gold-looking puppy pushing bread and a peanut butter jar across the top of my kitchen table. So I yell, 'Hey, what the hell are you doing?' I know this sounds funny, but right then I thought I heard a woman's voice saying, 'making a sandwich.'"

Harriet covered her phone and said, "Your old buddy is outdoing himself this time."

"I looked everywhere, no woman," JD said, "so I figured I'm hearing things."

"Did you find out how she got to your place?" Eddie asked.

"Never did. I even went over the next day and asked Little Oak, Big Icicle's all-around fortune teller. She said only that Zelda had a very far-away look in her eye."

Speaking of eyes, Eddie thought, *I must have that same look about now.*

"You know me, Ed," JD continued, "I wouldn't send you anything without checking it out."

Again, Harriet covered her phone, "Checking, hell! He probably asked some snowplow driver if he'd seen the dog."

"So," JD said, "I asked this snowplow driver if he'd seen the dog."

"What did he say?" Eddie asked.

10

"He said 'no,' but when I mentioned the far-away look that Little Oak had noticed, he thought the signs pointed to Arizona."

Turning aside, Harriet said, "They never should have let South Dakota into the Union."

"So, I'm up here with more dogs than snowbanks and I'm thinking with the grit this girl's got she'll shorten each day of Ed's married life by at least one disagreement."

"Eddie," Harriet said, "the man will never be well."

"And after years of talking about getting a puppy," JD said, "you now have the only dog in North America that makes her own sandwiches."

And talks about it, Eddie thought.

Bless Harder

Chapter 2

A month after Zelda's arrival, the assistant pastor at Saint Cecelia's, Father Ragone, stopped in on his way back from lunch at the Knights of Columbus Hall. He giggled as Zelda washed his face, and then with a special invocation, he placed her under the protection of "Roch," the Patron Saint of Dogs. "Hey," Zelda said quietly to Eddie, "tell the Bingo King I'm not signing up for the Ladies Guild."

When Harriet jokingly asked if the "Rock" insurance package covered homesickness for Big Icicle, the young cleric responded, "You won't need it. Do you know what they're doing out there this January morning?" he asked. "They're re-heating frost-bitten people in microwave ovens."

What Eddie and Harriet needed most was a special protection for the vegetation in their backyard. The commercial repellants that Eddie bought to prevent Zelda from destroying small trees and shrubs were not repellants at all; they were actually incentives. The big yellow print on the containers that boasted, "works every time" should have read, "If your dog's name is Zelda, get your money back."

The drip system, that life-blood of domestic plants in Arizona, had no choice but to leak wherever Zelda chose to chew. Other items that the Graces wished to protect–furniture, rugs–they stored in the guest bedroom. A miracle, duct tape, temporarily saved two glider cushions. Harriet concluded that it wasn't a good year for dog blessings and perhaps they should contact a conflict-resolution specialist.

Featherizing Healthcare

Chapter 3

As spring was about to arrive in Arizona, the sun must have wondered what it was supposed to do for a backyard full of dead and dying shrubbery. Desperate to rescue his favorite tree, a young Australian Willow, Eddie called his Big-Icicle friend, JD, for advice.

"Hey Cowboy," Zelda interrupted, "Do you want to know why there are no doctors in Big Icicle?" By then, Zelda was talking nearly as much as most wives, but only to Eddie.

"Not right now," Eddie said as he dialed JD's number.

Zelda asked, "It's about the dead willow, right?"

"I don't think it's dead. Harriet thinks it is."

"Before you get him on the line, there's a famous doctor story around Big Icicle that says a lot about JD; want to hear it?"

When nobody answered after six rings, Eddie said, "Okay, but hurry."

"I think it was around 100 years ago," Zelda began, "when a farmer near Big Icicle had a rooster that escaped from the coop every morning but loved the place too much to run away. He was an ordinary bird–chased hens and crowed in the morning–but he just wouldn't stay locked up anywhere.

"One February, according to the story, this farmer got the flu and went to see his doctor. Short on cash, he paid the doctor with the rooster and a promise of half of a small turkey at the following Thanksgiving. But when the rooster ran back to his farm the next day, the farmer pinched himself and said, 'Hey, I paid my doctor bill yesterday and I just got my money back.'

"Another pinch and the farmer had a racket to make all crooks giddy–he rented out this chicken to sick people. These people gave it to the doctor for his services and asked him to spare the poor thing's life for a few days. The doctor put the rooster in with his flock of chickens but the bird always escaped and ran back to his home farm."

"This is pure fiction," Eddie said.

"Not in Big Icicle. Listen, that little trick worked perfectly several times during that flu season, but as the farmer was about to discover, there's a risk in entrepreneurship.

"Later that spring, a deputy sheriff was driving casually around the countryside looking for a place to fish when he saw this rooster running beside the road. Seeing no farmhouses close by, he got the bird into his car and gave it to the first person he saw. Well that person happened to be one of the "chicken gang," and when the deputy seemed suspicious, the fellow begged for immunity in exchange for the name of the man who hatched the scheme. The sheriff subsequently fined the farmer fifty bucks and the deputy dusted off his tackle box."

Eddie, hiding his impulse to laugh, asked, "Is that the end of the story?"

"Not quite, there's a moral to it."

"And what would that be?"

"The moral is, 'never run *afowl* of the law.'"

"Good God," Eddie said, "but why are you telling this to me now?"

"Because your friend, JD, has a line of talk that would choke a bull moose and you're asking him to help you save a tree."

"He knows trees."

"Yeah," Zelda said, "like he knows airplanes. He knows one

15

grows leaves or needles and the other flies around and that's it."

"You'll see in a minute," Eddie said.

"Oh," Zelda said, "I forgot two important things in the story. One, there are no doctors in Icicle anymore because they moved to places where there are no chickens."

"And what's the second thing?"

"The owner of the rooster was JD's grandfather; he was slippery."

"How would you know?" Eddie asked.

"Hey, JD himself says the truth is boring; the world has too much of it."

Eddie nearly forgot why he was calling JD but he dialed again and clicked on the speaker phone.

"Of course, JD can't do much harm now," Zelda said, "after all, the tree is dead."

"Hello, JD, Eddie here. Is this a bad time?"

"No," JD said, "I was just trying to sing "Faded Love," that Country classic. How do I hit those high notes in the chorus? But that can wait, Buddy. What's up?"

"I got a Willow tree that looks dead but I'd like to save it."

"Is it all brown and ugly?"

"Well, Harriet thinks it is but I don't."

"How are you and Harriet getting along?"

"Just fine. I asked her to hold off on the tree for a month, but she says it has to go."

"You got Johnny Rodriguez's phone number? He sings "Faded Love."

"No, JD, I don't. Right now I need to save a tree."

"Ed, you've always been a big worrier. I'll bet Harriet doesn't sweat long over a tree, does she?"

"No, she doesn't," Eddie said, "and I worry about that."

"Okay, then I'll tell you what I did last year when my little American Linden tree got frost bitten."

"Listen closely," Zelda said.

"I walked up real close to it and said, 'please Brownie, don't go; you're so young.'"

"He also talks to airplanes," Zelda added.

"What happened?" Eddie asked.

"I learned that breathing life into dead things is not a man thing; it's a God thing."

"Did you dig it out?" Eddie asked.

"Well, no I didn't. You see, I'm not married to Harriet."

"So there's a guy who's really unbalanced," Zelda said, "and you're tilting a bit yourself right now."

Eddie disregarded that and thanked JD for the advice.

Zelda continued, "I love the way you solve problems. Usually, you go to that room full of books that you're so proud of, and when that doesn't work, you go to JD."

"What's wrong with that?"

"Just this: you're going from a burial ground for dead ideas, namely philosophy, to a gimmick salesman who begs a tree to rise from the dead. That's what's wrong with that!"

Instead of offering a rebuttal, Eddie thought, *I've got a 66-year head start on that dog; how did I get so far behind?*

Don't Do The Math

Chapter 4

From the beginning, Zelda displayed some practical survival skills, the principal one being "raid where you can and cut a deal where you can't." She had no qualms about either offering or taking a bribe, and like many young dogs, she learned or forgot according to the profit margins. She answered the "can-you-pee" question correctly the moment a sliver of Wisconsin Colby Cheese became part of the bargaining. Without adding a treat, calling her was like calling cabbage.

Zelda came ready to lick everything–hands, clothing, the top of Eddie's head when she could reach it. A single licking might continue for three minutes and then be repeated five minutes later. That habit meant lots of washing, which drove Eddie to implore, "Please stop licking everything! We're running out of soap."

Eddie's victories over Zelda were small and infrequent, more accidental than designed. Through it all, he played kid-gloves coach more than sergeant major and accepted minimal progress because the neighbors kept saying, "She's just a puppy." But puppyhood aside, Eddie confronted Zelda one morning on the patio. "We need to talk," he said, "that is, if you're not all worn out from sunning yourself on the glider."

Eddie brought no bribes to this meeting.

"You are six months old," he began, "that's one half of one year. I, on the other hand, am 66 full years old. Follow me now, that makes me 132 times older than you."

"So?"

"So what happened to age as an item for consideration when rights and duties are in play?"

"Pure folly," Zelda countered. "You have as many rights as you can get, and if you can't get any, you have the right to cry."

Eddie played a second card.

"Instead of tearing up the yard, why don't you meditate for a few minutes each day? It lowers your cholesterol and prevents strokes. The saints rarely have heart attacks."

Zelda yawned.

"Or try being dull. If you need a role model to help you with that, I'm here. I have expertise in the dull area."

"Go kiss a cactus."

Next, Eddie reminded Zelda that she had three beds, namely two large pillows worthy of any Las Vegas hotel and a premium airline crate, whereas he, a married man, had only one half of one bed. With a heart as cold and hard as the granite in the Black Hills, she fired, "With this argument based upon largely irrelevant math, your bed-counting and some nonsense about rights, what are you going to do next, circulate a petition?"

Eddie then advocated bipartisanship, the brotherhood of land animals and a sense of proportion as things they might build a relationship upon. That ended with Zelda's "Oh my;" and when Eddie asked, "Oh my what?" she said, "Oh my butt," and took a lap around the yard at Daytona-500 speed.

Despite the lengthening string of defeats, Eddie had always believed that time would eventually become the equalizer–meaning that when Zelda turned one year he would be just 67 times as old as she. But then, as happened so often in Eddie's arguments, when he carried his point to the punch line, he either had trouble following himself or there was no punch left. The future did not look promising.

19

Later that evening, Eddie mused, *Once my backyard over-flowed with serenity. It was a place where a man could evaluate world events, re-align his perspective without distractions. But all that's gone now and I am basically a homeless person in a yard that I no longer recognize, trying to sidestep a 30-lb animal that threatens to dislocate my kneecaps.*

Actually, debates and musings like these were of little importance since Eddie had already been infected by that famous "dog-people's disgrace," where the owner surrenders all rights to time and property and pleads, "Do anything you like (Zelda); just let me pretend that I am in charge."

The Dwindling Of Truth

Chapter 5

Zelda didn't volunteer a lot of information about her family history. When Eddie eventually asked about her roots, she reverted to the same mechanism that humans have used for thousands of years–she found a story, a folktale to explain her start-up. Like other accounts of the beginning of things, Zelda picked an area well off the main road (possibly in the southern highlands of Turkey) and let loose a yarn that couldn't be refuted by an historian or a scientist or the genealogical equivalent of a car fax.

"One evening very long ago," she began, "the dogs gathered for their annual conference. A clear moon watched silently, a million locusts sang their love songs and each delegate expressed his complete confidence in a new beginning with opportunity and prosperity for dogs everywhere.

"But then, instead of addressing critical issues like a dwindling food supply and public safety, this male-dominated group killed nearly a week talking about the latest Babylonian perfumes, the scarcity of upscale housing and old girlfriends."

"Sounds like conventions everywhere," Eddie said, "but go on with your edited history."

"Finally, an elegant dog with a beautiful gold coat yelled out, 'shut up' and then proposed a six-month moratorium on talking."

Here Zelda interrupted her tale to say that she gave the hero a particular quality to match that of the story teller—a common strategy among folklorists.

"So the dogs stopped talking?" Eddie asked.

"And they never talked again. In no time, the dogs discovered what everybody today knows—nobody likes a noisy dog. Their self-imposed silence made them extremely popular throughout the dog world, and as they became popular, the whole problem of finding food vanished. And because they no longer needed to hunt, they had lots of free time to look at quiet lakes and mountain streams and butterflies. And they could take six naps a day without worrying that an outside faucet was left running.

"In a few hundred years, just like with people, this habit of not talking became a custom, and again like people, the dogs came to believe that their new silence was natural, possibly ordained by a higher power."

"This sounds very familiar," Eddie said, "but you're still making it up."

"Hey, every songbird's got something to sing about. Every salesman and absolutely every politician is in the same game; it's called "upgrading the truth" to suit personal convenience. So yes, I've got a story, but is it so different from the one about Manifest Destiny that Americans have been living with and singing about for over 200 years?"

"Okay, you've made your point. Is that the end?"

"Not quite," Zelda said, "there's another point, especially for you."

Eddie said, "I might have known."

Zelda said, "This self-imposed silence was actually nature's way of protecting dogs against a long, noisy death from constant talking. Which brings about the big question: Is your hearing problem just nature's way of shielding you from constant verbal abuse? Is it another signal, like sleep, that helps you to stay alive?"

The whole thing might have ended with yet another win for Zelda, but mysteries and tall tales were like Biblical callings for

Eddie; they had to be pursued.

"So why don't you talk to everybody, instead of just me?"

"Simple, I chose you the same way Harriet chose you–from what was available. No mystery, no magic. You were on hand, so to speak, the way Moses and Franklin Delano Roosevelt were on hand when they were needed. Hey, God, politics and throwbacks work in mysterious ways."

"You're dead wrong about Harriet and me. Every week we say if we live another fifty years, we want to spend all of them together–a sure sign that we were meant for each other."

"Oh yeah, didn't you tell me just last week that, whenever two married people live in the same house, one of them always wants to be outside?"

"That was a joke."

"Tell it to Harriet and see how loud she laughs."

Zelda brought her big guns to any debates. "To return to the point, if you tell anyone that I talk and the TV news people hound you 24/7 for an interview, I will not speak another word. I'll just howl as they bag you for the institution."

Zelda's threat to turn him over to the "white coats" erased any chance that Eddie might open up to friends. Fr. Ragone believed in miracles but not in a four-million-year throwback that talks. And more important for a lifelong peacenik like Eddie, most hot-button issues were never on the table.

Eddie believed that all arguments over rights and values are worn out long before they can be resolved and yet there is an infinite variety of victories that each contestant can claim from those skirmishes. He therefore reached a quick resolution to his wins-and-losses problem; one that not only couldn't be refuted but one that would give him a victory in a widened sense of that term. In his new-found pathway to success (victory), Eddie said to himself, *Zelda wins everything. She sleeps where she wants, tells stories she knows can't possibly be true and threatens to expose me to public ridicule if I tattle. But wait, things could be worse; JD could change his mind and want her back.*

23

Age Spots Keep Falling On My Head

Chapter 6

To introduce Zelda to life where 90 percent of the people are from outside Arizona, Eddie took her to the Cactus Wren Café in Hearts Landing. There she would see what sunshine, discretionary funds and a constitutional right to freedom of speech can do to retirement. She would find that fun there always outranked organization and that answers often had little to do with questions.

When they arrived, Slack, a former Oklahoma truck driver, and Yancey, a Nebraskan known as "*Papa Grande* of the Sand Hills," were already slouched in their chairs for what they called "subcommittee hearings."

Gus, the owner of the Wren, served food "good enough to eat" and paid the help well enough to legitimize the sign above the cash register, "Work here and you won't have to live with your mother anymore." To support his business principles, Gus regularly bought supplies from the local thrift stores and played to his customers' sense of proprietorship by inviting them to leave usable, autographed chairs at his place.

Sahara, a new waitress at the cafe, was tall, quick witted, dark haired and round where roundness counts. Her personal accessories made every male customer remember the exact hour, place and weather report the first time he saw her. Slack, like foolish old men everywhere, longed to know where Sahara was from, as though he could go there and get one like her. Unsuccessful but persistent, the Oklahoman repeatedly offered to triple his pledge to the Save-Arizona's-Water campaign if she would go dancing with him up in Tombstone. "Hope," Sahara cautioned, "is a valuable tool but it should not be abused."

Gus was more interested in what Sahara brought to the cash register than where she came from. When customers asked about her, he smiled and artfully dodged the subject–citing privacy. "However I will tell you this," he said to one inquirer, "when she and I were talking about the job, she was able to follow and answer a two-part question. So I'm positive she's not from anywhere around here."

With the steady flow of re-settlers from outside the area, Gus's restaurant flourished. In this regional melting pot, the cafe became a care center for those who survive on pipe dreams that are either forever gone or forever on the way.

Yancey, one of the few within striking distance of good sense, loved formless squabbles over rights and duties the way football coaches love their opponent's end zone. He didn't walk as far as he did a decade earlier but he could still put his pants on without leaning against something. Those who knew him agreed that his mind was more alert than most of those who get themselves called "leading experts." He was a well-disguised 76-year old.

Going straight at old ideas was Yancey's favorite sport. He questioned all opinions and theories not directly supported by the unsentimental hand of physical data, and daily offered his own try-out answers, meaning "let's try this out and see who yells loudest." He cautioned against following the Ten Commandments without first reading the fine print. On one occasion, the lanky Cornhusker took on the immensely popular assumptions that humans are free and that this freedom of choice gives them a supremacy over the animals. On one occasion he asked, "If a mountain lion stalks a deer and a man stalks a mountain lion, how do you know that the man is free and the lion is not?"

"Hey, my main man," Yancey greeted Eddie as he and Zelda joined him at the usual table. "How's your new friend doing? She looks smart."

"I know she's energetic, and she really likes water," Eddie was happy to get questions. "She sticks her whole head into her water bucket every day. Her bark sounds like a typical woman's voice, which means with my difficulty in picking up higher frequencies, I don't always hear her that well."

"I know all about your problem with female voices," a woman nearby said. "My husband got that shortly after we were married."

Wren customers were never shy about offering personal assistance. A middle-aged woman said, "I saw a little gadget on TV last week that they said would turn your hearing problems around immediately or your money back." Her husband beside her suggested hypnosis.

Slack asked the woman if she had seen any new products that would broaden his peripheral vision and added, "Right now I can still see two full-figure women at the same time, but if they could kick that number up to say three or four, I'd be interested."

Zelda quietly congratulated Eddie for pursuing intellectual stimulation in the most unlikely places and then turned her attention to a small family birthday party at one of the tables. The honoree, an 87-year old man, held up the only gift that he had permitted—a rescued and retouched black and white picture of himself and a group of Kansas farmhands standing beside a threshing machine some sixty years before. A noticeable tremor notwithstanding, he raised the framed photo the way a man might raise a glass of burgundy and said, "It's funny how much more important things like this become when you get older—and how very child-like everybody else at this table looks. Thank you very much."

As the applause subsided, a Medicare-eligible woman returned to the health problems from a few moments earlier. She announced that she had put all of her problems squarely into God's hands many years ago.

Yancey, true to his habits, wanted to know how that transfer was accomplished.

"Well," she said, "this is embarrassing but here goes. It happened at my tenth high school reunion. The disc jockey was playing "Whole Lotta Shakin' Goin' On" by Jerry Lee Lewis. We were all dressed up, dancing and shaking, but I happened to shake once too often."

"What happened?" Slack asked quickly.

"The worst," the woman said. "A very essential strap on my evening gown snapped."

"Then what?" Slack again.

Sahara, the round waitress, stopped still and stared straight at him. "Give it up, Slack. There is no *best part* to this story."

"Let me just say that I wasn't as *protected* as I had been a moment earlier and I ran off the floor even before my husband could give me his coat."

"Were there any eye witnesses?" an anonymous customer asked.

"Yes, there were several witnesses–with very big eyes."

Zelda thought, *I'm guessing here but this woman seems to enjoy telling this story.*

"I'm missing something," Yancey said "What's the connection between your snapped strap and your problems?"

"Just this," the woman said, "At that moment I saw that I would never be strong enough by myself to avoid a crisis like that. So I made a promise to God that from then on I would listen for Ilis word and follow whatever plan He had for me."

Yancey asked. "Did God take the deal?"

"He certainly did!" the woman answered. "And I have had total peace of mind ever since. A great glow has come over my whole life; you could call it a sneak preview of heaven." Then she asked Yancey, "Wouldn't you like to glow like that?"

Yancey paused a moment and said, "Well, since I've never been to heaven and I'm not much of a "glow" guy, right now I'm leaning toward 'no.'"

Men Of Principle, Mostly

Chapter 7

First off the following morning Zelda asked, "Is that all there is in that café, old bucks with loose hinges?"

Eddie said, "Okay, next time I'll drop you off at the library; maybe you could read a biography of the inventor of nail polish. Those men are my friends."

"How'd you choose them?"

"I chose them because they were here,"

"Well give Big Ed the star for that."

"They might not be all slick and shiny, but they have principles, like honesty and fair play. If they take a job, they do it."

"They didn't pay for those principles, I hope," Zelda said.

"No, they didn't. They worked hard all their lives and the principles were a bonus. Don't forget, it was people like that who got you on the plane between two South Dakota blizzards last December."

"Where did the Oklahoma guy learn how to sneeze?" Zelda asked. "If he honks like that in your house, he'll shatter the pottery."

"No need to worry, Harriet wouldn't let him in the door."

"Actually, you fit right in with that bunch. You were lying like a congressman about the baseball games you claim you got paid for, the crowds, and the stories in the paper. I'm surprised you didn't say Jackie Robinson wanted your autograph."

"I never lied once."

"Maybe not, but you forget easily," Zelda said. "About that out-of-work chiropractor you said fixed your arm? One minute you said he charged a hundred bucks; two minutes later, you said two hundred. Your bookkeeping stinks."

"A hundred was with the team discount. Two hundred was the regular price."

"Okay, weren't we talking about this dump restaurant we went to, what was it, the Wobbly Wren or the Prickly Pear?"

"The Cactus Wren. The Prickly Pear is Sahara, the waitress. If marriage comes up sometime when we're there, you'll know why they call her that."

"So we're in this place," Zelda said, "close and friendly as you see it, and you tip the "Pear" person five bucks for carrying a six dollar sandwich out to your table."

"She's single and probably going to night school."

"The sign said Gus pays his people well," Zelda said.

"He does."

"There are plenty of businesses that don't. You're not working. Instead of bankrolling one waitress, why don't you talk to the chamber of commerce about setting up an educational fund for high school drop-outs?" Zelda was getting more fun out of the Wren than she cared to admit.

"I talked to a group of low-income people a number of years ago."

"So you got only one speech in you? How many people were in the audience? Three old cranks and a dog, like yesterday?"

"As a matter of fact, there were nearly 200 people there."

"Whoa, Cowboy, if you're talking about that speech you gave on upward mobility, Harriet says there were 39 people there, not 200, and nobody petitioned anybody to re-name the library after you."

"Okay, okay," Eddie said, "so I'm a tad high on the number;

29

there was a nice crowd."

"So who was actually there?"

"Well, some part-time faculty and a lot of secretaries and maintenance."

Zelda liked that. "Who wrote your speech?"

"I wrote it–and practiced it."

"And what did you say, after you got all practiced up?"

"I said people running copy machines or garden rakes start 30 yards behind in a 40-yard race, and that makes winning pretty tough."

"Clever! What else?"

"A lot, but what I remember best was the old guy who told me he was tired of hearing people like me telling him to prop up losers. I can still hear his last line, 'let them pull themselves up by their own bootstraps.'"

"And what did you say to that?"

"I said I was born with white middle class bootstraps and they were easy to pull."

"I must say, impressive. If the money's right, I'll go along for your next speech and try to look interested."

"I'll reserve a front seat for you."

"Meantime, could we find a better cafe? A million people in the Tucson area, there must be a diner where they wash the windows."

"The fancy places are 45 minutes away, and they don't take dogs."

"Okay, then I'll have lunch tomorrow right here on the glider. See your neighbor's vine hanging over the wall?"

"Yes."

"It makes a very tasty salad," Zelda said. "I'll have that with a dab of blue cheese."

30

Matrimonial Side Effects

Chapter 8

The next time Zelda and Eddie pulled into the Wren, Slack was holding up a picture of a full-figure woman in a seriously-shrunk swimsuit. Proportionally, the woman was the Northern Hemisphere and the suit, Rhode Island. Pointing to the subject's upper body, Slack said, "You know what would happen if one of those fell on you? You'd be out of business–a goner."

Eyeing the picture, a customer nearby offered, "Well, whenever you think you're about to get hit, call me and I'll run right over and take your place."

Sahara grabbed the picture, dropped it on the customer's table and said, "Here, add this to your Slack collection."

The customer looked again at the picture and said, "If she ever moves to Tucson, I'm canceling all of my appointments."

"Maybe you don't know it," Slack said looking around the group, "but I was a full body scanner before they had airports."

Sahara hissed disgustedly, "Tell me, was it the red dirt in Oklahoma or the unrelenting wind that made you obsess about sex?"

"Actually I think it's numbers," Slack answered. "Example, last week I was reading about the national debt and sure as hell, the second I saw all those big numbers I was right back to women again. Don't you ever think about men?"

"I do," Sahara said, "and right now I'm thinking about husband number three, Lionel. He looked forward to doomsday, not because he wanted to see people blown up but because he wanted to play reporter and show off his total recall of each casualty's final two minutes."

Zelda thought, *You can really pick 'em.*

" And when it wasn't doomsday, it was bad news for dust. He not only vacuumed every closet; he vacuumed every piece of clothing in them."

A gentleman nearby asked, "Would that have been a Hoover or a Dirt Devil?"

Slack snickered and mumbled, "She must have her bra on backwards."

Sahara wasn't finished with Lionel. "One day for lunch, he opens a family-size can of soup and asks me if I want part of it."

"I said 'I'm hungry, about half,' and then he disappeared for 15 minutes. He was reading the labels on every can of soup in the cupboard."

"Very thoughtful," another stranger said.

"So finally Lionel asks me if I want vegetable or beef tips."

"Vegetable," I said. "Then he asked if I wanted mostly carrots or potatoes."

A woman close by said, "If he's in the continental USA, I want him."

"So I said, somewhat louder, 'just heat the soup,' and what do you think he said next?"

"He was running for president?" Slack guessed.

"No," Sahara said, "but close. He asked if I wanted the top or the bottom half of the can."

Zelda thought, *Hey he's looking out for your every need.*

"I threw something at him, maybe a tea strainer, and ran up the stairs."

"I hope you didn't hit him," Yancey said. "A serious injury from a strainer can end a man's presidential aspirations."

Sahara wound this up, "Then he wanted to know if he had

said something wrong and where was I going. I yelled, 'I'm going to the bedroom where there isn't any damned soup!' So counting Lionel and two other tries at marriage, a pink flamingo in the front yard sounds a lot better than a fourth husband in the house."

When somebody snickered, Yancey looked up from the morning paper, "Hey, no laughing, we're talking quality suffering here."

Anxious to draw attention to the quality of his own marriage, Eddie said, "I've heard Harriet say several times how I was "there" through all the ups and downs."

Sahara was merciless, "She meant you were in the way!"

Eddie turned to Zelda, "Well, what did I tell you about Sahara and marriage?"

A woman in an Arizona Athletics T-shirt said how the mercy rule in softball could teach you something important about wedlock. When a customer looked puzzled, she said if one team leads by eight or more runs after five innings the game is over.

Sahara said, "Get a flamingo; they don't eat soup."

Slack, who never married, saw another option, "What Sahara needs is a 70-year-old trainee? I just got two new crowns and I throw a mean gutter ball."

Zelda thought, *And he comes with his own gate belt.*

"I'll bet you can do the 10-yard crawl in 20 minutes flat, right Slack?" Sahara asked.

Yancey reported reading that people engaged to be married in New Guinea exchange shoes for three months before taking the plunge. The practice supposedly serves as a public reminder that the couple's best days are behind them.

Slack turned the clock back. "I almost got married once. I was 18, standing outside the pool hall in Coyote Bend, Oklahoma and this girl in short shorts was sitting on a bicycle half a block away. She was stretching one leg out to touch her toe on the sidewalk. If she'd stayed there another two minutes, I wouldn't be here today."

Big applause.

Just then a Tucson dermatologist ordered a cup of coffee and sat in the chair with his initials, "E W" on it. Sahara greeted him with, "Dr. Ernest Wells, I presume. You look so much richer than the last time you were here."

Sahara told Yancey that the esteemed doctor's "annual take" after loopholes approached a million bucks.

Yancey, the cynic, said. "Offer him a free sugar cookie and tell him he's saving Tucson's hide."

A woman with a small dog at the counter said bubble baths are known for saving rocky marriages.

A man eating a burger wasn't so sure, "You don't have much to work with there–just you and the bubbles."

Eddie and Zelda left when Sahara appeared ready to lay into Dr. Wells about spiraling medical costs and patient rights.

"With all respect to Sahara," Eddie said, "even if a new wife finds the bathroom closet full of her husband's shoes, she probably shouldn't ask him right off how many feet he's got."

"Well," Zelda said, "before you start on whose fault it is, have you noticed that 80 percent of the dog walkers in Hearts Landing are women?"

"I have."

"And even when their men are walking with them, the big boys are talking and playing know-it-all and the women are still handling the leash."

"So?"

"Real sicko yesterday. This dude is walking with his wife and a terrier and, believe it or not, this time he's holding the leash. And this time what do you think the wife has in her hand?"

"What?"

"A poop bag–used!"

Sunset

Chapter 9

A newcomer to the ways of her human cousins, Zelda didn't make issues bigger or smaller than they were; they already had a size of their own. But like her distant relatives, her judgment occasionally failed her.

Thus, one November morning when Eddie made his semi-annual visit to Honeysuckle, an assisted living home, Zelda walked in without thoughts of the residents there as either a national treasure or a burden on working taxpayers. If they looked weak and scared, that was because they were weak and scared. If they had a conversation with someone no one else could see that was a consequence of time and physiological breakdown. She saw how important basic comfort was to those in declining health and hoped federal resources wouldn't run out.

Then Zelda made a very quick judgment. She announced, "When I don't know who I'm talking to and can't scratch my butt because I forgot where it is, I'm out of here."

Eddie didn't laugh. Instead, he gently patted her shoulder and said, "It's easy to be sure when you're not well acquainted with your subject." He reminded her that the residents at Honeysuckle had simply worn out some of the tools of personal management and they faced each day with the strong possibility that no visitors

35

would knock on their doors.

Zelda saw the advantages of having been to the facility before.

The staff at Honeysuckle kept things clean and airy, and called those they served by their preferred names. The card players hated losing but they didn't throw things when they lost. The lemonade tasted like lemonade.

Zelda wondered what those seniors had done for a living, what games they taught their kids and grandkids. Nearly four score on average, the years had made them more alike than different. They all needed their meds, several naps per day and a regular dose of the good old days.

Helen, a three-year resident with a knack for invention that compensated for her memory loss, cornered Eddie for 10 minutes while Zelda lay stretched out in the sunshine. When she referred to her boyfriend's recent visit, Eddie stood as tall as his five/nine frame allowed and said, "Helen, if I hear that lout's been hanging around here again, I'll come over and beat him up." The truth was there hadn't been a male in her life since Bill Clinton was the governor of Arkansas.

Zelda liked the absence of loud noises at Honeysuckle–you could hardly hear the garbage disposal. The Grace's neighborhood suited her well but the occasional booms and bangs of work trucks and garbage cans could startle her.

On the way home, Zelda said, "When I'm old, I hope you will tell your buddies how I made your life exciting and complete."

"If I can also tell them why our backyard is barren," Eddie answered.

"And I hope I don't pee in the house just because I forgot to go to the door."

Eddie assured her, "I'll take you to the door if you forget."

Be A Man! Scrub One Handed

Chapter 10

When Eddie awoke on Flag Day, Zelda said, "Let's take a walk." Her tone said, "this is a business meeting."

"I see you're using a smaller cup for my food," Zelda began.

"To be honest," Eddie said, "I hadn't noticed." Not noticing cup sizes was no surprise. Eddie ate virtually all of his meals at home for four decades but could never remember where the spoons were.

"Well notice please that you're giving me less and less food and I'm getting hungrier and skinnier."

"Okay, I'll look for a bigger cup."

"And I'm getting tired of walking the same old route every day with the same old hounds sniffing me."

"Of course," Eddie said, "and I've had dill pickles shoved at me for 40 years, so get used to it."

"If this sniffing continues, I want to renegotiate my benefits."

"To be clear, you, my canine friend, are on an entitlement program, 100 percent of which is funded by me. And how do I get thanked for that? You look away half of the time when I'm talking to you about something of substance."

"You mean like your six-minute explanation of why round things roll better than square things? Oh, that's real substantial and every college should offer a major in it. You're paranoid. You accepted me from JD in order to keep your mother-in-law from moving in."

"You're way out of line here."

"To the contrary, a month with that old lady and you'd have begged the waste processing plant for a part-time job."

"For your information," Eddie said, "my mother-in-law is a kind if not gentle woman. She's a little hard of hearing is all."

"So hard of hearing that when she turns on the TV, the house plants curl up."

"I can live with that," Eddie said.

"You hate noise so much you never ring a doorbell; you tap three times on the door with your index finger only."

"I'll talk to her sometime."

"You're afraid of a 90-year-old lady who can't hear a chain saw."

"That's my business, not yours."

"Then set your wife down and have her straighten the old girl out," Zelda said.

"How totally naïve you are. There are no known records of married women being "set down" and "straightened out" by their husbands."

"Your problem is you can't stand up to anybody but me."

"No, no. The real problem here is I don't have enough ear wax; I can hear you too well."

"Everybody knows you went down and stayed down after that "D" in zoology 45 years ago."

"The professor couldn't believe I had no interest in trichinosis or sheep liver flukes."

"And I don't like all these orders either," Zelda said. "You give me orders just to have something to do."

Eddie reminded Zelda that her pulling on the leash had made his left arm half an inch longer than his right (exaggeration) and she in turn reminded him of their agreement to let her be a dog 99 percent of the time.

"And before you bring up the backyard again," Zelda said, "can I help it if you buy expensive trees from some fraud over in New Mexico called 'Backyard Magic' and half of the leaves fall off before you get them to Tucson?"

"You stripped the trunks bare."

"They were dead."

"I think you should remember," Eddie said, "in matters of reason and logic, I am the one here with the degree in philosophy."

"Your problem, not mine," Zelda said.

"I have over two hundred earned credits," Eddie said, trying to salvage something.

"And you must have needed every one changing that toilet seat yesterday," Zelda said as she steered the conflict closer to one she was certain of winning.

"I just happen to believe," Eddie turned almost solemn, "that bathroom maintenance does not automatically fall to women."

"Almost noble, and you will be forever known as the son of Tidy Bowl. But look, take some comfort from knowing that with only two people in the house, you have a 50/50 shot at being the first one to use that new wrinkle-free, bottom-loving toilet seat."

"And I'm not embarrassed to say that I know the difference between standard and industrial strength cleansers."

"And long after you've scrubbed your last bathroom, Cowboy, some admirer will visit your grave on Memorial Day and place a can of Big Wally there in your honor."

Eddie almost smiled at that.

"And finally," Zelda said, "here is the most important point of all for you who are forever trying to figure out if your life has a purpose. Listen, 40 years of cleaning bathrooms won't tell you the secret to life; it won't even tell you why you're not a Popsicle. But you will know exactly what to do and how to do it if you drop a juicy little orange Popsicle on your tile floor."

Spit They Weren't Using

Chapter 11

"If you're the type that falls asleep easily, don't go to baseball games. If, on the other hand, you like comedy, go often." That comment by a stranger decades before, broke Eddie's heart. Although he was just a second-stringer on his high school team, Eddie considered the official baseball rule book more important than the Charter of The United Nations.

Eddie's love of the game survived his inability to play it well. At twelve, he was badly coordinated, at 15, he still couldn't "hit a lick," and later as a third baseman, he trembled whenever a beefy batter threatened to slam a hot ground ball his way. Away from game action, he fantasized about being carried off the field with his glove raised above his head and the crowd cheering, "Eddie, Eddie." With a passion like that for what some have called the greatest game ever invented, he didn't take in spring baseball games in Tucson to sleep or make jokes about the way hardball is played.

To add to the excitement of being around professional ballplayers, Eddie chose the annual Bring-Your-Dog-To-The-Game for an afternoon around America's "pastime." Big league baseball, combined with her skill at catching a Frisbee and the chance to meet some of her own kind seemed like a winner. The weather report for that March Saturday was favorable–low 70s, zero chance of showers.

When they arrived 20 minutes early, the playing field was filled with dogs chasing rubber baseballs and barking at each other. A pair of older fans noted the similarities between certain dogs' agility and that of former baseball greats like Saint Louis Cardinal shortstop, Ozzie Smith and the Giants' Willie Mays.

The ceremonial first pitch–thrown out by a restaurateur who donated a slice of pizza to each of the first 500 fans–came and went without applause from Zelda. What amused her most was a woman with a man, not a dog, on a leash. The fellow's collar said "Louie" and his impersonation of a Bassett Hound caught enough attention to get the pair 20 seconds of TV time later on the evening news. Zelda's first impression of baseball was, "there's more fun in the stands than on the diamond."

The home team eventually took the field, expecting to outdo the dog act and impress the modest turnout of paying spectators. But when the second baseman muffed a high-hopping ground ball and then kicked the thing as he tried to recover it, a low-tolerance fan to Eddie's left yelled, "Hey, you with the gold glove, have you thought of taking up soccer?"

In the home half of the fourth inning, a batter hit a fly ball that the wind picked up and dropped just over the short right field fence. This number eight hitter in the lineup started pumping his right arm toward the crowd as soon as he rounded first base, and then as he crossed home plate, he pointed in the general direction of the only cloud overhead. Eddie felt obligated to tell Zelda that exhibitionism of this kind unfortunately detracted from the game.

"Why is that fellow in the white circle swinging his bat viciously at nothing?" Zelda asked.

"He's loosening up," Eddie answered, hoping that would satisfy a newcomer to baseball.

"Well, if being loose is important, some of these beer people up here should be playing."

Once in the batter's box, the hitter dug up a good part of the ground around home plate with his spikes, re-laced his batting gloves after each swing, and spat twice as if to mark his territory. The fourth pitch, a 60-mile-per-hour change-up, hit the batter in the back. This brought a visit from the team trainer who supervised a minute of recovery before okaying the player to stay in the game at first base. Once there, he unloaded the remainder of the guards and wrappings worn to prevent injuries and gave the first-base coach plenty of time to pat him warmly on the shoulder.

Zelda was curious. "Where," she asked, "is this athleticism, this superior eye-hand coordination and the quick thinking that you said were holding America together?"

Eddie pretended to be studying the program.

The batter with the bruised back kicked the first-base bag twice and re-arranged the gold chain around his neck.

"What's going on now?" Zelda asked.

After a long pause, Eddie said, "They're going over the signs."

"What Signs?" Zelda asked. "Signs of life? Where's the medic, now?"

From their seats behind first base, Zelda continued to needle Eddie, "I think the runner is lost. I swear I heard the coach say, 'Now Ernie, when you get to second base, take a sharp turn to the left—you'll run right into third base." Eddie was rescued by a raucous woman who attracted nearly everyone's attention by holding up a large sign inviting Ernie to an all-night wedding chapel.

Like a lot of never-has-beens, Eddie enjoyed comparing modern players' self-aggrandizement with "the way we did it." He said back then the players had no enhancing apparel and very little spit that they weren't using. He hated to criticize but he said in the old days the "hotdogs" were at the concession stands and if you wanted to know who was winning the game you looked at the scoreboard. He stopped short of saying exactly how old those days were.

Zelda's interest rose when an old fellow asked Eddie if he knew Bob Feller.

"Farm boy from Van Meter, Iowa," Eddie said proudly. "He

came to Tucson all those years for Cleveland's spring training but, dumb me, I didn't even come out to get his autograph. That's not right." And Eddie meant it.

"That's too bad," the fan said. "I'd give you the ball he signed for me, but I only have the one."

"That was really dumb of me," Eddie stressed.

"They say batters couldn't actually see Feller's fast ball," Eddie's immediate friend said. "All they could do was listen to it as it went by at 100 miles an hour."

Zelda thought, *There's a 49-year-old joke coming here.*

"In a game in Saint Louis in 1946," the Feller fan went on, "Bobby was setting those Cards down as fast as they got to the plate."

"He could do that," Eddie agreed.

"In the fifth inning, a Cardinal batter took a called strike one–which he didn't see, of course."

Eddie winked at Zelda to say, "I told you this would be fun."

"So Feller winds up for the next pitch. The ball goes swisssh, and the ump calls strike two. The batter didn't like the second call one bit, so he turns around to the umpire and says, 'that sounded a little low.'"

When the Bob-Feller guys split off for the men's room, an upper mid-life woman in a severely-worn Oakland A's cap added her commentary on modern baseball.

"Have you noticed," she asked Eddie, "how many kinds of pitchers they have these days? Before this is over, they will have run enough of them out there to fill a schoolyard. They have job descriptions like middle reliever, long-term reliever, holder, set-up man and closer."

Eddie knew that an excess of pitchers, coupled with pinch runners, pinch hitters, defensive specialists and replacement players for those who'd been ejected made baseball labor intensive, but he wanted to hear the woman out.

"Starting pitchers," she said, "used to pitch the entire ballgame–even doubleheaders, way back. These days, they have so many relief pitchers running on and off the field that it looks almost like the dog show before the game."

When "God Bless America" came over the public address system in the 7th inning, Zelda asked, "Is God curing the players of the exhibitionism you mentioned or is He just sterilizing the spit?"

Knowing the futility of trying to answer that, Eddie thought, *And to think we used to play this game for nine innings, with just nine players and the promise of a free case of Pabst Blue Ribbon from the Beer Shack, afterwards. I don't recall anybody spitting at an umpire. But to be honest, the case of beer was one of the reasons why we had only nine players.*

In the top of the ninth, Ernie, the player who Zelda said had asked for directions to second base, came to bat a fourth time and learned how often bad luck follows incompetence. When the umpire called a strike up around his neck, he walked out of the box and kicked more dirt–and spat again. When the umpire then called a third strike, a little off the outside corner, the batter outdid his earlier performance. He sprang into the air, landed within six inches of the official's chin and jerked his head sharply downward several times. His outburst was accompanied by a volley of phrases, none of which sounded like "Good Buddy." The official, mask in hand, responded quietly. "This is an exhibition game, but you don't have to exhibit your worst behavior." Zelda said it was all quite ugly and wished the red-faced brute would be sent somewhere for treatment.

Eddie pointed out that such protests are not uncommon when a player thinks he's been victimized by poor officiating and asked Zelda, "Suppose an umpire made several bad calls while you were batting, how would you handle it?"

As if to add a hotdog and fries to her fun, all at Eddie's expense, Zelda ended the afternoon with, "Well, first off, I would walk slowly up to the umpire and then I would say, 'Gosh, Mr. Umpire, I'm so sorry you couldn't see that the last pitch was nearly out of the ballpark. I do hope you're not having serious eye trouble.'"

Hold On To Your Hanky

Chapter 12

Everywhere along the early-morning walks, BMW drivers and yard crews alike stopped to admire Zelda. In early December, one elderly gentleman actually came down from the tree where he was stringing Christmas lights just to admire her grace and bloom.

When the temperature dipped into the 20s, the number of dog-walkers also dropped. Zelda suspected it was the owners' aversion to comparisons between her and their animals, not the weather that kept them indoors. When Eddie questioned that, she challenged him, "How many women would ask for your autograph if you were standing next to George Clooney?" On one particularly cold morning, one of the "shiverers" interrupted his stroll to say, "On days like this, hell doesn't sound too bad, does it?"

Those daily treks produced, Harold, Zelda's first boyfriend. He was in truth a handsome 10-year-old Black Labrador with the demeanor of a Presbyterian minister. Zelda ignored the age difference and offered Eddie a deal, "Take me to his backyard for a weekend and I'll give you the movie rights to my life." Unfortunately, Harold "went home" within a year and Zelda turned again to showing off at bus stops and working anyone who might have a treat in his pocket.

The daily ritual also produced Opal, a mature dark-haired

woman who made old men plan their walks around the precise times and places where they had last seen her (Not one of them knew the breed, size or color of the dog Opal walked). A cocked 30s hat and her runway stride brought new life where there had been none for thirty years. Indeed, one of her admirers felt so rejuvenated one morning that he asked her where she was from. With a cool not seen between the Canadian border and Tucson in a century, Opal responded, "People think I'm from Vegas–and playful. Well let me tell you, Handsome, I'm *not* from Vegas"– leaving the question of "playfulness" open.

It's difficult to walk anywhere around Hearts Landing without running into Mesquite trees. They outnumber evangelists and telemarketers combined by at least eight to one. Their pods soon became Zelda's favorite fast food and she devoured them with the efficiency of an overweight midnight-snack king.

Zelda made only one exception to her instinct to eat as much as she could as fast as she could. When Eddie held a miniature Milk-Bone between his teeth–show time for the trail audience–Zelda came slowly to within an inch of his chin and gently removed the treat. In all other instances, she grabbed, chewed and swallowed treats in one continuous motion.

The folly of chomping before you check showed the day a female jogger offered Zelda a top-of-the-line cookie while holding a small hanky in the same hand. In a heartbeat, both biscuit and hanky disappeared. For days the woman called to ask if Eddie had "seen" anything. Finally after a dozen inspections, the tiny hand cloth reappeared. Everybody thanked God, but nobody asked the owner if she wanted her hanky back.

Yancey, Eddie's grassland friend from Nebraska's panhandle, won the competition for Zelda's affection, hands-down. This came easily because she liked people with at least a minimal interest in truth and suspected anyone who claimed to have a lot of it.

A cosmic analyst without a college degree, Yancey was old but he was his own man. He could love Bluegrass, ragged clothes, new or old friends, without apology or pretense. He didn't wear glasses because he said he hadn't seen anything that he wanted to see any better. He epitomized what natives of the Sand Hills call the "ripening time," that is, when thoughts of what worked either poorly or not at all took a turn for the humorous.

Each summer, Yancey drove a thousand miles northeast until he found grain fields, singing windmills and other signs of his "alma mater." Had this prairie-born wise man ever decided to run for public office, Eddie would have been first in line to volunteer for campaign work.

Re-distributing The Marbles

Chapter 13

Harriet knew that sending Eddie on errands beyond the single mall in Hearts Landing meant he might have to ask a policeman how to get home. She always kept the stops to two easy-to-find places so he could get back to doing the same things he had done yesterday and the day before that. After some last-minute wifely counsel, Eddie took the short grocery list, slid a watch in need of a battery onto his left arm, grabbed a package to be mailed to his sister, Beth, in Duluth, put Zelda on the front seat of the Volvo and headed out.

Traffic in "Hearts" is never heavy, but at the first stop sign Eddie didn't just glance and go. He studied the area–front and back, left and right, all mirrors and windows–and then took a second look to confirm the findings of the first. After eight minutes of driving five mph below the speed limit, he arrived safely at the first stop, the United States Post Office.

Eddie took Zelda and the parcel for Beth–Harriet's award-winning peanut brittle—into the waiting area, grabbed a number and stood a few feet behind the last customer in line. He had forgotten that PO policy permits only service dogs inside the building until an ill-tempered fellow pointed to Zelda and barked, "Is she a tax payer?"

Eddie apologized for his mistake and then said to Zelda, "Never be unfriendly; let someone else be that."

"See the "held-mail" sign and that female in the hat standing by it?" Zelda asked very quietly.

"Yes."

"She's got you in her sights."

"How do you know that?"

"They all go for guys with that slow-and-wounded look."

"Maybe I met her somewhere," Eddie said as he saw her maneuvering for a better angle.

"You can do a lot more than mail packages here," Zelda said. "Maybe you could even get engaged."

"I'm not worried."

"Better be, Cowboy, this isn't her first hunting trip."

"Maybe she's new and wants to say hello," Eddie said.

"Yeah, to you," Zelda said. "This is *a*-HARMONY – "a" as in Arizona Blunt."

The Postmaster yelled out two more numbers, which put the huntress in position for a shot.

Zelda warned, "It's *High Noon*."

This veteran of the chase was efficient. She gave her name as Kate, her age as three score and two years and slid close enough to read the time on the watch that was running on Eddie's arm. And then, hurrying like a hunter suddenly running out of daylight, she popped the question, "Is your wife alive?"

The world's understanding of divine intervention was never as clear as the moment the Postmaster yelled Eddie's number. He dashed to the window, asked the clerk to hurry and bolted like a scared rabbit, leaving Kate to conclude that she had wasted valuable PO time on game that couldn't be bagged.

Looking for shelter fast, Eddie didn't count his change or pick up his receipt. Neither did he look back until he was safely out of range inside Dingle's Food and Drug.

Zelda said, "Maybe next trip you should add a cane or cough every 10 seconds."

Eddie scanned the area around the pharmacy counter the same way he had searched for traffic at the stop sign. Having satisfied himself that no one but the white-coat guy could hear him, he gave the purpose of his visit—the colonoscopy package.

Predators, however disguised, habitually select the weakest game, and this raider of privacy was no exception.

"So, they're going to take a little look around, huh?" the pharmacist asked with no particular interest in the matter. "Let me know if they find gold and I'll have them check me out."

Eddie wished the man would keep his inside jokes inside.

"The store just expanded the greeting card section especially for needs like yours," the predator offered.

More than ever, Eddie wanted to keep moving.

Placing the supplies on the counter two minutes later, the druggist said, "You're in business. You got the mix, the sweetener, plus two pages of directions."

Zelda said, "This dude is a throwback to mushrooms. Tell him he will be on your mind during every minute of the procedure."

Eddie said, "I don't want to engage an unarmed man in a battle of wits, so let's grab the groceries and go."

Eddie had long believed that, based upon the number of spats that occur when married couples shop together for groceries, he should set up a booth in Dingle's for peace talks.

He understood that, regardless of the outcomes, all parties begin each new shopping ritual with unarticulated vows of good will and compromise. In that spirit, Harriet had always handed him his list of items, shorter and less complicated than hers, and they went their separate ways to find them.

In a matter of moments, Eddie spotted a husband and wife in need of an arbitrator. They were at the stage of the food hunt when the items in the husband's cart were supposed to match those on the list that his wife had given him.

The pair stood next to the deli counter where Dingle's kept a cute little bell that customers could ring if they received outstanding service. But this couple wasn't there to ring the bell; they were at that level of disagreement that's often followed by, "I guess I should do everything myself." Something didn't match. The issue was the difference between what the wife had listed and what the husband had in the cart. Each party was serious and occupied with winning, but judging from the wife's general intensity, Zelda said this was actually a "one-member board of inquiry."

The argument appeared to center on red dots that, according to the wife, were supposed to be on the snack packages. She pointed repeatedly to the bags while the husband pointed to his list. With the outcome still in doubt, the wife took a very purposeful step toward her opponent and demanded, "Norris, what did I just say?" Just for fun, Eddie walked over and rang the little bell.

Moving on quickly, Eddie went over his own list. Thankfully, there were no foreign foods, no "one-and-done" items for the bathroom, no ice cream that might melt if he got stopped by a law officer. Anticipating a quick trip with only a few purchases, he put Zelda in the front of the cart.

Big mistake. Within five minutes, they encountered a tall woman covered with silver and turquoise and looking like the president of something. She stared critically at Zelda in the cart and asked, "Oh, are puppies on sale? I must go back and get one." From that moment on, Eddie made no eye contact with anyone until he was at the checkout counter.

There, he put his six items on the conveyer belt and placed the divider bar squarely behind them. As he tried to remember if this was credit or debit and which colored button to poke, the woman behind him asked, "Aren't you going to pay for my groceries?" Now, how does a man answer that question? Wasn't his 20-dollar donation to summer camp enough?

"I don't think so," he said, "why?"

"Well, you must have plenty of money; you're wearing two watches."

Wondering why everyone wanted to embarrass him and trying to change the subject, Eddie asked the woman how she liked the results of the recent election. "Listen, Mister," she said, "when I

51

was preparing for this little shopping trip, I asked a much more important question than any politician asked during the entire campaign. I said to my husband, 'Leo, I'm going to the store. Do you want peanuts in the shell or in the can?'"

The next stop was the jewelry counter at the far end of the store. There were no senior females lined up this time; just one burly customer making a heated complaint to a saleswoman.

"You know, this place is so dumb," the man at the counter charged, "I'll bet the manager–where'd you say he is, in Alabama?–doesn't even know the definition of "nine," does he?"

The clerk, a moonlighting woman experienced in dealing with unhappy customers, added a pinch of humor to the question. "It's unlikely that the boss reads up on the definition of nine very often, so if you will define nine for me, I'll see that he gets the information immediately–in Alabama."

"Look, Dearie, the first definition of nine in my dictionary is 'one more than 8.' Look it up–and tell that to Alabama."

Eddie needed this kind of delay the way a baldheaded man needs a barber but he suffered through it.

"And while you're there, in the dictionary, see if you can find a word that describes your right to jerk me around over a watch battery."

"I'm not sure there is such a word," the clerk said.

"Of course there is," the man said. "The word is Capitalism. And what it means is, 'money talks, in court, in politics, even in little Hearts Landing."

"I'm sorry," the clerk said, "we replace watch batteries only for customers who buy their watches here. There's a liability risk involved that the store does not wish to take."

"You might not know this either, but this is Memorial Day weekend," the hefty gentleman went on.

"I'm quite aware of that. My kids marched in the parade this morning."

"You see that flag waving outside? My granddaddy was in WWI, my daddy was in the Big One and I got this damned cane free of charge from Korea. We all fought like hell so you could be free to sell jewelry, and watch batteries, to anybody who pays for them."

"We appreciate that every day, but maybe you could get your battery replaced downtown."

"I'll bet I could get it replaced in Buffalo too, but I'm not going to New York. And I'm not spending $3.70 on a gallon of gas to get downtown just to restart a damned watch. I'll buy an hour glass; hell, somebody's got to stand up for something."

The clerk tried again. "We have several very good watches that are fifty percent off for Memorial Day. You could get one at a great price and avoid this problem in the future."

"Do I look like I got a problem? You got the problem–you and this dude behind me. He's got two watches on one arm."

By this time, Eddie wanted to help.

"Excuse me Sir," Eddie said, "if you need a few bucks, I could..."

Uncertain of how long this might go on, the saleswoman looked first toward Eddie, then back at the angry customer and broke in, "I'm sorry, I have another customer."

Not remembering where he had bought his own watch but sympathetic to the veteran, Eddie said, "Thank you, but I'll get a battery at some other store."

The clerk deadpanned, "I hear there's a big sale on in Buffalo."

As the man began walking away, Eddie said. "Pardon me Sir..."

"Oliver!" the man said.

Eddie kept trying, "I think I understand your frustration."

"I think you don't. You see, there's a little game going on here. I'm doing a non-punishable, guilt-free deception. It's the key to staying alive in the free market."

"Oh," Eddie said, "you mean you told a lie about your family's military service?"

"Not a lie at all. I used a "patriotic disguise;" the football coaches call it "misdirection."

"Pretty fine distinction."

"Listen, Mr. Scout's Honor, don't lecture me on the uplifting effect of telling the truth. Tell me that the truth will get a battery in my watch–one this store says it sells and I am ready to pay for."

Eddie concluded that Oliver was not ready to rethink the need for honesty. When he and Zelda left the store, Oliver was at the customer service counter, pointing to the flag.

Eddie and Zelda never saw Oliver again. When they were in the store some weeks later, Eddie inquired about him. Customer Services gave this account: Oliver returned a week after his failed attempt to replace his watch battery and bought a handsome watch at the sale price. He said his grandson was doing volunteer work in Indonesia and because of the annual rainfall there, 68 to 78 inches, the life of watch batteries is short. The assistant manager threw in 10 extra batteries at half price, suggesting that volunteers like the grandson need everybody's support. Later, Oliver returned the watch, saying it gave him "dermagraphia," a reddening of the skin often caused by rubbing against certain metals. The store manager gave him credit for the watch; the extra batteries never came up.

"So Mr. Philosopher," Zelda said, "how does something the size of a watch battery become the cause of such frustration?"

Eddie said, "My Friend, the short answer is, 'everything is relative.' A slightly longer answer is, 'since the world, as it is, lacks the capability to make everybody rich and happy, there is a continuous fight to re-distribute the marbles.'"

54

She's Trying To Kill Me

Chapter 14

Those who knew retired Minnesota judge, Rex Horne, swore he could irritate a sandbag. He interrupted every speaker without regard for dignity or right of way. No one ever recalled Rex saying, "My wife, Agnes, is a remarkable woman." What they remembered was, "For a woman, Agnes is remarkable." A week after Rex broke his ankle he hobbled into the Cactus Wren. When a sympathetic customer asked if the accident had actually happened on his wedding anniversary, the Judge responded, "Yeah, it was a rotten day all around."

On another of his stops at the Wren, Rex made the near-fatal mistake of criticizing Sahara's love of Dixieland Jazz. He bragged about his collection of Beethoven and Stravinsky and suggested that the basic "noise" of Dixieland could be duplicated on a slightly-modified oil can. Sahara, not one to waste time or energy on Rex, said, "The only reason you want me to like classical music is so I'll be like you. Well, I don't want to be like you, you boob."

When the large Maple tree in Rex's front yard cast a protective shadow on his neighbor's car, His Honor scoured legal precedents to see if he could charge the neighbor a fee for using his tree's shade. The neighbor compared him to an appendix–more trouble than he was worth.

True to form, when Rex joined Eddie and Zelda in the park on a late-March afternoon, he began, "Hey Billie, still hanging around with Rover, huh?" (Rex also had a habit of forgetting names.)

"Rover!" Zelda growled.

"Has he learned anything, yet?" Rex asked.

"He!" Now Zelda really didn't like him.

"Yes, she has," Eddie said, "she knows not to trust judicial types from Minnesota."

"Well that's not much, but you were smart getting a dog instead of a cat. Ever try to cut a deal with a cat? You can't do it."

Eddie said Zelda was a quick learner.

"You know," Rex said, "watching other people is the best way to learn things."

Zelda thought, *This is wondrous indeed. Expect a CNN news crew to be here in half an hour.*

"No surprise I suppose" Rex said, "but I learned how to be funny just by watching funny people."

Zelda walked to the end of her leash and murmured uncontrollably.

"The secret, however, is watching the right people," Rex went on.

Tolerant Eddie listened without asking anything

"Example, my ex-wife, Agnes, always bought the groceries, okay?"

"Okay."

"Twice a month that included milk and Wheaties."

"Hummm."

"Then the next day she'd buy two dozen donuts. So, now we have milk, Wheaties and donuts."

Eddie wanted to say "So?" but remembered that questions were never really meant for Rex.

"So now we eat Wheaties while the donuts get old and rocklike. Agnes was copying a very bad habit from somewhere."

Eddie hung in.

"For three years I tried to get Agnes to watch me and other

people who are good at saving money on groceries. It didn't work; she never noticed."

"Sorry to hear that."

"Then I saw how she kept bumping into things around the house and I tried, for example, staying clear of standing lights and candy bowls, thinking she'd do the same."

"That failed too, right?"

"Big time. She bumped right into my Mediterranean coffeemaker with a picture of Hidalgo on it and smashed it to hell–135 bucks."

"Well, I don't know, Rex. What's a dead coffeemaker if it keeps a marriage going?"

"Ah, it's good you said that, because it gets me right to the point I want to make. I think she was trying to kill me. She read a lot of mysteries; she knew how to do it."

"Agnes? You're kidding."

"No way. You see, she's twelve years older than I am and everybody in her family died young, so she figured she'd die before I did."

Zelda thought, *Death can be good.*

"So what does she say to me every three days? She says, 'when I go, you go.' She didn't say how or when either of us would go, but I guessed the rest–something added to the Wheaties."

Now Eddie couldn't hold back, "Did you hide the Wheaties?"

"Didn't have to. She ran off three months later– July 4th, Independence Day."

That evening, just as Eddie was settling in for the Arizona/ UCLA softball game, the phone rang.

"Willie, Rex here. I got one quick question for you."

"Shoot," Eddie said listlessly.

"Those little yellow flowers we saw today, do you call them wildflowers, one word, or wild flowers, two words?"

Eddie had what he thought would get Rex off the phone, "I don't call them anything; I just look at them."

"Well Ed, it seems to me that a wildflower, one word, is a

particular flower out in the wild, whereas wild flower, two words, is the name of any flower that happens to be growing in the wild."

"I wish I could help you but all I know is they give me hay fever."

"Well, do flowers get their names from the place where they're growing or do they have their own names wherever they are? Tell me that."

"Have you tried googling it?"

"Well, if strange flowering plants sprung up in your back-yard," the judge said, "what would you call them? One word or two?"

"Rex, we haven't had a single flower in our yard since Zelda got here."

"I wish you knew more about this so we could have a longer conversation."

Not a chance in hell, Eddie thought.

"So if a flower is called a wild flower because it grows in the wild, is a flower called a dead flower because it grows in the cemetery?"

"Rex, maybe you should ask somebody in the cemetery."

Don't Remember, If You Can Forget

Chapter 15

Before Zelda turned two, she and Eddie had walked more than 800 miles, the equivalent of a round trip from Tucson to Las Vegas. It wasn't always "Blueberry Hill" but Zelda no longer changed directions every two steps and Eddie was free to enjoy the Arizona sunrise, to remember/daydream aimlessly and to praise all other dogs as well-mannered dog owners should.

But that new freedom did not cure Eddie's chronic hearing problem as he discovered one foggy April morning when he greeted a fellow dog walker. The walker, a woman looking worn out by her unruly animal, glanced hurriedly Eddie's way and mumbled, "What a crappy fog!" Eddie, heavily influenced by his new commitment to praise every dog he met, understood her to say, "What a happy dog," and gushed, "And so is your dog." Later, when Eddie discovered his mistake, he took a private oath to rethink his need to be a well-mannered dog owner.

Unless you take your morning walks on the fourth floor of a Hilton Hotel, April in Arizona means watch for diamondback rattlers. Encounters with them in the wild create both wonder and caution in most pedestrians. You can argue about whose land it is or who is the nuisance in the desert, but dog walkers soon learn that poisonous reptiles can be game-changers in a broad sense of that phrase.

Long before Eddie had familiarized himself with diamond-back habits, he had inadvertently knelt down beside one, stepped over another and came within a handshake of several more. During one of the lighter moments at the Wren, he said the federal government should require all rattlers to wear orange hunting vests. In the same spirit, Zelda replied, "Another government regulation? The democrats will love it."

Eddie got serious about snakebites each time he remembered how he lost his 11-year-old companion, Rip. It was 9 o'clock on a July evening in 1991 and the old dog had stretched out on the patio of the ranch home that the Graces had built near the college where Eddie taught. When Rip hadn't moved for 20 minutes, Eddie went out and found two tiny punctures in the tip of his nose. He and Harriet stood quietly together, stunned by the mysterious union of beauty and horror in the natural order. He carried Rip's body to the garden where he buried it by the lights of his pickup.

• • •

Many of the sidewalks in Hearts Landing are close enough to the houses that a pedestrian passing by can hear TV sets and telephones. Sometimes, Eddie and Zelda could make out small homey sounds like breakfast dishes and toasters coming from kitchens. Then one Saturday morning the sound that Eddie least wanted to hear came roaring through an open window–the cruel hum of a vacuum cleaner sucking the very life out of its owner.

For 40 years, Eddie had pushed and pulled and dragged big heavy vacuum cleaners over living room floors, around furniture, up and down short ladders. Cleaning jobs of any kind irritate a man who hopes to do all housework from a sitting position. That irritation doubled after Zelda arrived and half of what the vacuum picked up was dog hair. When Eddie complained, Zelda reminded him that nothing had been said about shedding.

That humming sound drifting across the sidewalk re-confirmed Eddie's belief that vacuum cleaners kill more fun than mothers-in-law and taxes combined. He blamed the manufacturers for not knowing that some of their machines would eventually fall into the hands of philosophers who are already overburdened by the very nature of their profession. He ranked awkward cleaning equipment just below the birth of Rex, the Minnesota judge, on the list of things that never should have happened. He immediately remembered how he searched the phone book for the number of a licensed witch to curse his enemy and added his name to the "Please-Call" lists at churches and synagogues.

Eddie estimated the annual cost of vacuuming: damage to home furnishings hit by the cleaner, $600, operating costs at minimum wage, $1,750, operator's rehab (counseling and red wine at five), over the top.

Sometimes, after he had finished cleaning the inside of his car, Eddie left the vacuum outside the house overnight, praying a needy person would steal it. One evening, he left it with a note, "Father Ragone forgives bigger thieves than you every week. Or, if you're uncomfortable with the formalities of confession, skip that step and just blame your sin on public education. Think of the greater good that will come to the current owner and by extension, to all those who know and love him. Thank you."

One day, pausing at a trail bench, Eddie asked Zelda's advice about his cleaning problems. "Cowboy," she said, "next time, stop vacuuming and leave the thing standing alone, running, so Harriet will think you're operating it. Then after 15 minutes, turn it off and shove it back into the closet." The idea sounded great, but Zelda didn't know Harriet the detective.

Eddie didn't really think that these recollections on the walks were driving him crazy. You're crazy if you try the same thing over and over, expecting a different result. Eddie was trying many different things and getting the same result. When he waited in doctors' and dentists' offices, he read *Good Housekeeping* magazine, not *Sports Illustrated*, thinking someone would ask why he was staring at vacuum cleaner advertisements. He wrote his congressman, asking him to recommend a federally-funded rehabilitation program for victims of acute domestic anxiety. A postcard two months later said thanks for the request, that the congressman's schedule was tight but that he was "following up on the matter."

Those who knew Eddie understood that not doing things was a bigger part of his life than doing things. Any "doer" on the block would grab the nearest vacuum, slam it from one room to another, cover up the nicks and scuffs on the furniture, take a nap and be ready for cocktails at five. Unlike the go-getter types who develop long lists of big things to do or love, Eddie was left to remember the pain inflicted by a lowly, lifeless vacuum cleaner.

One day when Eddie's trail reflections shifted from things he hated to things he regretted, he told Zelda of the time just before she arrived when he dismissed two door-to-door missionaries. "I didn't intend to be rude," he said, "but when they asked if I had been born again, I told them I had been born once and that Mother had said that was quite enough."

"Look at it this way," Zelda said, "you could have told them to get lost."

"Well, I almost did, but in a different way. I said, 'You know, I think you might be committing a sin of pride here by assuming that you know more about running my life than I do.'"

"Oh, oh," Zelda said.

"And do you know what happened next?" Eddie asked.

"God showed up."

"No, He didn't, but I did another dumb thing. When one of them asked if I wanted a brochure, I shouted, 'hell no!'"

"And you're regretting that?" Zelda asked.

"Well, they were just kids. Maybe I misunderstood when they seemed to say, 'spend a little time with us and you're guaranteed a soft landing in heaven.'"

"Don't you have a things-to-do-again list?" Zelda asked. "That's where I'd put this born-again story."

"If I had taken the brochure, I could have called them to apologize," a worried Eddie said.

"You've got to toughen up, Cowboy."

"Maybe so," Eddie agreed, "but meanwhile do you know why I tell you this stuff?"

"Of course I know! Because you're full of guilt and I'm on a leash."

"I'm sorry, I have to follow the leash law," Eddie said, "but you'll be relieved to know that I am ready to quit telling stories all together—no more about things I hate or regret or anything else."

"Oh, thank God! See there, one visit from the missionaries and you're better already."

"I'm quitting mostly because I hate being interrupted in the middle of a good story. From here on I think I'll mail my jokes to people. That way, I can pretend they're reading them and I won't get interrupted."

"Interruptions can make anybody want to give up story-telling," Zelda said.

"Now get this. About the same time that I had this encounter with the missionaries, I was at this funeral. The old man's death was no surprise so it wasn't one of those big crying events. At the burial site, everybody was standing around as the mortuary staff took some extra time getting the casket out of the hearse. So with the delay, I thought an amusing anecdote about the guy would be okay. I was almost at the punch line, 10 seconds, max, and you know what happened? They suddenly yanked open the back door of the limo, pulled out the coffin and just like that my story was shot dead–interrupted by a *corpse!*"

"Hang on to all your stories until the body is six feet under," Zelda advised.

"It wasn't a surprise or shock," Eddie said, "like if the dead guy suddenly reared up and ordered a beer; that kind of thing would stop a presidential address. The body was just lying there, waiting to get some rest. But no, not even a crowd of mourners could wait for five damned seconds while I finished my story."

"Try bartenders next time. Even if they haven't heard a word you've said, they know when to laugh and when to say 'absolutely.'"

"Now I'm not a man to hold a grudge," Eddie said, "but at my funeral, I want an official to move my coffin just a foot or so right in the middle of somebody's story."

Zelda, impatiently awaiting her turn, suggested, "Look, you're growing a record-setting ulcer over nothing. Why don't you just tell people that you don't like being interrupted?"

"I tried that, once!"

"What happened?"

"I got interrupted!"

Give My Regards To By-ways

Chapter 16

Every September, Eddie wished he was a duck. Not one of those fat wobbly "quackers" on city ponds, but a wild, stately bird, gliding and bobbing with the currents of the Missouri River. He never understood why a composer somewhere in the Dakotas hadn't written some serious duck music. On each return to the Heartland, Eddie sat on the Nebraska side of the river just below Lewis and Clark Lake. There, like a first cousin of Nature, he watched the waterfowl and embraced the beauty of fall on the Plains.

All things considered, Eddie was sure that wild ducks add elegance and beauty to their neighborhoods. They paddle and strut their importance but they're not pushy or rude. Like pastors of churches, they are in the business of offering comfort and perspective to the needy. If the area gets crowded, they just fly off to the next available waterway to comfort somebody else. Forty years away from Middle America had not dulled his excitement over waterfowl on gently rolling streams, never mind that fall on the prairie is only a brief pretext for the wind and snow that follow. And so when Zelda turned three, she, Harriet and Eddie set out for the land of their birth and a special stop at Zelda's first home, Big Icicle, South Dakota.

65

A car trip from Tucson to the Central Plains charms those who grew up with native grass, grain elevators and two-lane highways that test a car's front end alignment. Eddie found splendor, even spirituality in that, but then he was in love with the region and every mile was homecoming. Zelda, not so indebted to the area for her outlook, thought he should get around a little more. Several years before, Eddie had asked Harriet (also not quite as stirred as he) if she thought he had been named for the eddies in the Missouri River. She responded, "Could be. Would you like to change your middle name to Flood?"

The anticipation begins just northeast of Tucumcari, New Mexico, where the land levels off and a good-sized jackrabbit can be spotted 300 yards away. Without frontage roads or the hum of traffic going by on both sides, it's easy to forget that you're actually getting somewhere. But none of that bothers those reared on nature and space. Nobody in the Volvo questioned the hard work and candor reputed to be second nature to the Plains people until Eddie took a good-faith turn at a billboard advertising what Handsburg, Nebraska, has to offer. The four-by-five sign showed a knife and fork, a gas pump, a bed and a cocktail glass. The large print at the bottom read, "WE HAVE IT ALL."

Three minutes later and two miles off of Highway 81, Harriet saw a second sign reading "Handsburg, Pop. 626." With only positive feelings about the area, Eddie didn't question the meaning of "all" back on the billboard. Harriet, to the contrary, wondered if some of Slack's relatives had moved north and gone into travel-related businesses. Articulated or not, they expected this 'all' to be a little bigger, but they smiled, got a ham and cheese sandwich, filled the gas tank and waved to as many as waved at them–which was everybody either in a pickup or on foot.

After three days of eaves dropping on storytellers in roadside cafes, visiting family and seeing almost as many churches as bars, the trio headed west to find Zelda's "home" town; she was giddy.

Eddie's imagination was in fast forward and the Volvo sounded almost new as it carried them across the Nebraska/South

Dakota state line and onto the Pine Ridge Indian Reservation. They stopped briefly at the small church that had once served as an emergency room for the victims of the massacre at Wounded Knee, then on to the site itself. After a few moments to remember the spirit of Crazy Horse and the Ghost Dancers, they pushed deeper into the land of the Sioux.

Northeast of Rapid City, the roads narrow (the sides, as the locals put it, get closer to the middle), the horizon lengthens and you better not have a Starbucks attack. But that's the Dakota story that Eddie remembered–open country and a population that lives by what it has, thank you very much. Everywhere, the people talked about jobs, theirs, more than foreclosures. Life, simple and often unforgiving, was still what it was before he and Harriet moved to Arizona forty years earlier.

Big Icicle didn't have much of a skyline. It boasted of no scrapers competing with the clouds for space, no beltway with drivers challenging each other for speeding room. Unlike the small Nebraska town nearly 400 miles back, there was no sign asserting, "We Have It All;" just "Big Icicle next," carved on a slab of pine lumber and hung from a tree.

A quarter of a mile farther, Harriet rolled down her window to ask a pedestrian where the center of town was. He looked puzzled momentarily before answering, "Let me see if I can help you with that. Now, your present location would be Big Icicle Boulevard." He then assumed a practiced "I've-got-you" look, grinned broadly and said, "There are no other locations."

Harriet was amused, but as they followed the dirt road to the "business district," her three decades with the FBI told her that even nothing can look suspicious. "What do they do here, Eddie? Think they run drugs?"

Eddie answered, "Somebody should market fresh bottled air; they've got a lot of it."

"Maybe I should make a phone call. You know, it wouldn't be the first time."

Zelda thought, *You can't investigate nothing.*

Eddie guessed they might be running snow or maybe pine needles.

"Very funny," Harriet said.

The widest street in Big Icicle featured one service station with one gas pump, a general merchandise store, a bar named The Melting Spot and a single-story lodge with a red sign on top, "Motel 2–Bring your own light." The "2" part specified the number of rooms available. Zelda loved it. The rest of the town could be seen with a single swing of the head.

Big Icicle had not reported a major crime in 40 years because, the part-time mayor said the people hadn't learned how to be crooks. Those who had been there most of that time urged the town council to charge a fee for touring "South Dakota's most successful social reform movement." Rush hour wasn't before or after work; it was any moment when two or more vehicles were moving simultaneously through the business area.

"There it is," Harriet said as she pointed to a one-by-four-foot sign reading, "JD Anderson, A Dog's Best Friend." Then as they pulled up in front of the house, JD himself jumped from the porch and shouted, "Zelda, my love. They treating you okay? You are the beauty I knew you'd be."

After a delay for dog talk, he asked the Graces, "How the hell are you? Need a jacket or something? You must be cold."

"We're just fine but the traffic out here is a killer," Harriet joked.

"Do you think we should string a rope across the road and call Big Icicle a gated community?" JD asked.

Harriet smiled when he looked skyward and proclaimed, "I hereby declare this fair city the property of Queen Zelda! Long live the Queen!"

Inside JD's slump block home, Harriet picked up a flyer, advertising "Open Enrollment for Dr. JD Anderson Lectures on THE MEANING OF LIFE …Limited Seating."

Harriet asked, "What are you going to talk about at these lectures?"

"First one, 'Little Known Secrets behind the Loving Cup.'"
Harriet looked used.

Zelda thought, *JD is always this way.*

"Ah, I see you don't like the cup idea," JD said. "What about, 'Six Quick Ways to Enhance Your Soon-To-Be-Naked Look?'"

Minimally interested but willing to play this out, Harriet asked, "So what's the connection between any of this and the meaning of life?"

"Eight dollars and fifty cents, cash money, no checks," JD said with a wink. "Tourists down in Rapid will love it. You see, a lecturer needs a hook more than an explanation. Ed here never hooked a thing with his theory of non-being, did you Ed?"

As Harriet groaned, Zelda thought, *Not another word, JD; she's licensed to kill.*

"No crowd I ever worked," JD said, "waited more than six seconds for details, much less proof."

"The nation's attention span is shrinking, that's for sure," Eddie said.

"Oh," JD added, "I'll be offering a few specially discounted meanings of life for only $3.95–all in three different colors and suitable for framing."

He then filled three glasses of his best domestic red and answered the question that Harriet wanted to ask about the town's name. "A hundred years ago this place had no name," he started, "so the big store sponsored a contest on the condition that the name should describe the town and the winner should get half a cord of firewood. Damned if two names weren't tied when the votes had been counted, so the mayor had to decide the winner."

"Interesting," Harriet said.

"After two days of discussions and a number of small cash offers," JD said, "the mayor gave the town its name. He chose "Big Icicle" because he said it sounded more genteel than "Freeze Ass.""

JD's bungalow had that single look. There were boxes of dog treats on the counter, a chicken cacciatore wrapper in the sink and a dust level along the baseboards that suggested he might not own a broom.

"Excuse me," JD said, "I got this damned bladder problem."

Eddie understood that.

"If it doesn't go away, I'm going to change my name to Darth Voider."

On the seat of the only serviceable chair lay a draft of another advertisement reading, "If you don't know whether your grandfather had a bicycle or a hairpiece, you need, KNOW YOUR ROOTS, Family Services."

Showing it to Eddie, Harriet smiled and said how she wished they knew more about Zelda's background than JD's story of her showing up in his kitchen.

Back from the bathroom, JD pointed to a small picture of Zelda at 12 weeks.

"Gorgeous dog," he said holding the picture where everybody could see, "especially with the hair and that little wrinkle in her one ear."

"People in Hearts Landing think her coat is almost as eye-catching as Arizona's Palo Verdes in April," Eddie said.

Another round of the domestic and JD was ready to tell how he came to know Zelda was special.

"It's that reedy Sioux woman, Little Oak, Big Icicle's seer extraordinaire," he said. "She's over at Motel 2; you probably noticed her place when you drove in. She looked at your girl at 10 weeks I'd guess and said, 'I see Arizona sunshine in her future.'"

Zelda was caught up by the reference to extraordinary sensory powers and JD wanted his friends to get a positive feeling about his Native American friend. "And the day I sent Zelda to you, Little Oak told me, 'you will see her one more time.'"

Eddie thought this was rigged but politely asked, "You mean she knows the future?"

"Just parts, not everything."

Harriet, a daily reader of her horoscope, asked about Little Oak's credentials.

"Oh, she has fantastic credentials, and strong genes," JD said.

70

"Her grandmother foresaw the election of Herbert Hoover six years before the votes were counted. Those poll guys could save a bundle during presidential campaigns with one call to Little Oak."

JD countered a skeptical look from Eddie with, "She gets messages the way Sitting Bull did before the battle of the Little Bighorn."

Eddie said, "C'mon."

"She hears Sitting Bull the way people who play the piano by ear feel their way through the right notes."

Then JD looked Eddie straight in the eye, "You play the piano a little, don't you?"

"I do. So?"

"She saw a piano keyboard the day we put Zelda on the plane."

"I don't believe this," Eddie said.

"You will later."

"Does she read tea leaves, or palms, or what?" Harriet asked.

"Icicles mostly. That's where she saw the piano, in the lines of an icicle."

Eddie had no plans to mention any of this in the same breath with Aristotle or John Dewey.

"No joke," JD said, "Lucky for you it was so cold here two weeks ago that even the icicles were frozen. That's local humor but watch out; those babies have something to say."

"Why doesn't she go to Vegas where the money is?" Harriet asked.

"Two reasons. One, Vegas doesn't have a lot of icicles, and two, the messages she gets from Sitting Bull travel better where there's no junk in the sky."

My Mother's Eyes Were Blue

Chapter 17

After six minutes of sightseeing along Big Icicle Boulevard, the threesome stopped in front of Motel 2 where Little Oak sat in a willow rocker on the front porch. Her Wrangler-based apparel complimented a smile that for years had kept the vacancy sign out of the window. Her body language said, "Maybe you don't want to arm wrestle this woman." When Eddie asked about a room, Little Oak rang the bell hanging from a rafter and said, "See if anybody's home."

Setting up for the night took Harriet only a minute because she wanted to know more about Little Oak's talent for seeing what's down the road. For the present, the descendant of Sitting Bull poured three glasses of a red wine, known in the area as Big I's Hair Thinner, and led her guests into an adjoining room that she very proudly called the tepee.

Inside, the bookshelves told the visitors that Little Oak read more than icicles–Tolstoy, *Death of a Salesman*, *Waiting for Godot* and the essays of Montaigne. Above Will Durant's 11-volume set on civilization, a faded sign read, "You don't like my medicine? Go to Walgreens."

After the Grace trio had settled, Little Oak pointed to the three small eye-level windows and explained, "The south window lets me look toward Wounded Knee; the west gives me a view of the sky leading to the Little Bighorn, and the north window, always open a crack, channels messages from the spirit of Sitting Bull."

One large eagle feather above the west window seemed to say, "Memphis has Beale Street, the Irish have "Danny Boy" and the Oglala Sioux have Crazy Horse."

"Why no east window?" Eddie asked.

"The soldiers came from the east. They took the sacred places and said, 'get over it.' I don't want to see any more soldiers."

Actually, Little Oak had made her peace with soldiers and westward expansion long before. Her tiny living quarters reflected only her desire to preserve the things she thought were important, Native American or not.

"You should know I don't speak in tongues," she said, "or fly around the room. I listen more than I talk and all readings are done privately. One day each week I don't talk at all. That clears my head for "calls waiting" from the north."

"When will you do the reading?" Harriet asked anxiously.

"Hmmm, reading and the motel business," Little Oak said. "You get a private room for sleeping and I get the tepee for any late-night deliveries."

Harriet wanted more detail but respected the owner's right to set the ground rules. Little Oak showed Harriet the way to the bathroom.

"She's her own shrink," Zelda said to Eddie, "I think she hears messages from Sitting Bull for therapy, the way others whistle or whittle and the way you watch ducks."

When the women returned, Little Oak poured the remainder of Big I's Hair Thinner into three blue "reading" glasses. Harriet, with curiosity and confidence growing, whispered to Eddie, "I'm hazy here but I think I'm in. My mother's eyes were blue."

Little Oak pointed to the high-back chair with its rich red upholstery, "Notice how the seat is worn from side to side. That speaks to the bodily proportions of the previous owner, an archbishop."

Zelda thought, *What mighty prophecies, benedictions, guilty verdicts and appeals for moolah must have emanated from that chair! And now a self-taught descendant of Sitting Bull sits on at least part of it, also talking about things to come.*

Little Oak said, "The white man's imagination made him judgmental; truth made Wounded Knee a troublesome memory."

For an hour the tepee was filled with talk of conciliation v. triumph, change v. status quo. Little Oak said, "Some of us are conductors, some are resistors. My forecasts do not bend to the convenience of either the distributor or the customer."

Harriet wished Father Ragone would take a vacation on the Northern Plains to balance all of his talk about New England and the Red Sox.

When Little Oak felt satisfied that the air flow at the North window was adequate, she arranged the red chair with a candle-holder and a light blue bowl. "I have been getting faint messages since you pulled your iron travois up at JD's "dog house." Traveling 1,500 miles to let a dog see the place where she was a puppy, you can feel the fellowship of life in that."

Eddie blushed with pleasure at the thought but said the trip also included a special stop at Fort Robinson, Nebraska, where Crazy Horse died.

To assist her in selecting the proper icicle, Little Oak asked Eddie and Harriet for their birthdays. Eddie's, April 4 and Harriet's, September 9 made a total of 13.

"But it's late, my Friends," Little Oak said, "I must ask for privacy. I hope you won't be kept awake if I play the guitar quietly. I don't play well, but music speaks a universal language."

A week on the road told Harriet sleep was good. Eddie loved all guitar players.

To reassure them, Little Oak said, "Privacy is crucial to successful reading, the way noisy participants are crucial to pep rallies. It's so quiet here you can take a nap on the big street anytime and never get run over. I heard that once from a guest."

Eddie asked when they would know the message.

"Dawn tomorrow, at Ghost Dance Lake. The lake's name is unofficial; it honors the memory of Wounded Knee. It's only half an hour by slow car. Sometimes I walk to it. On special days, I swim across it–you know, like I'm getting baptized."

Outside, Eddie asked Zelda, "What do you think of her?"

"Well Cowboy, I don't know. She might be a fraud, but tonight she's our fraud."

"I'll bet she gets good tips," Eddie said.

Unfortunately, the night's rest that the Graces had looked forward to turned into six hours of searching for reasons why a seer/listener would spend an evening discussing long-standing ideologies with strangers and then spend the next morning somewhere in the timber charting their future. What Native American builds a house with no view of the east because "trouble comes from the east?" What motel owner takes two strangers and a dog to an out-of-the-way lake without charging a fare? At one point, around midnight, they imagined Little Oak answering their questions, "You take what you can from life; it hardly makes sense to pursue something that you cannot have."

Harriet seemed to be nearest the answer when she recalled how her uncle Albert drove visitors to the corners of his large ranch in western Nebraska just to show them grass, birds and the places where deer ate their breakfasts. Little Oak, like Harriet's uncle, saw value in preserving the past for the future.

Let Buffalo Roam

Chapter 18

The Grace's night-long search through the complexity of Little Oak ended at six a.m. when she gently tapped on their door.

At seven, they stood on the shore of beautiful Ghost Dance Lake–clear, cold and untouched by either earth-moving equipment or bug repellant. It was home to the ponderosa pine and the Black Hills white spruce.

On the south bank, Little Oak kept a canoe just big enough to take Harriet and her to the lake's center. Zelda was miffed at not being invited but she settled for some free-style splashing 10 feet into the water.

In about five minutes, Little Oak stopped paddling and turned to Harriet. "The buffalo don't roam anymore, but the spirit does. A message from Sitting Bull came through the North Window last night. Today, I will give you half of it, three simple words. You will recognize the second half later–when it comes to you."

Harriet instinctively reached for a pen.

"No need to take notes," Little Oak said. "You will remember. FBI, right?"

"But how will we know what the second half of the message means or what we should do?"

Little Oak said, "When you were sixteen and your mother told

76

you to follow your dreams, you didn't expect her to have one for you in her pocket, did you?"

She's avoiding the question, Harriet thought.

"The message will come in little words," Little Oak said, "words like 'I love you' and 'please don't walk on the grass.'"

She then took a piece of buffalo skin smaller than a playing card from her shirt and pressed it into Harriet's hand.

"As the icicle melted last night, it showed three sections," Little Oak said. "The top was murky, the middle turbulent, and the last part, smaller than the rest, was still and clear."

Harriet's eyes darted nervously toward Eddie, then to three mallards moving quietly along the far shoreline.

"You are coming into a period of stress, then to a test of courage that will in turn leave you as serene as Ghost Dance Lake."

Little Oak turned the buffalo skin over.

Harriet stared at what she would later call part of the Indians' Bill of Rights.

"The back side," Little Oak said, "is for your half of the message. Within three years, you will hear it and then you will bring it to this place."

Harriet didn't ask where and how because she was becoming sure that, in matters like this, Little Oak acted on her own or not at all.

"Three," Little Oak said, "is a very important number. In at least one of your religions you proclaim three gods in one, the trinity. Your culture celebrates three wise men in a Christmas story, not two or seven, three. In your national pastime, you have three strikes, and three outs. Your children learn about the three bears and the three little pigs."

Harriet studied Little Oak's message and then, in a slow, ghost-like whisper pronounced each of the three words, "let buffalo roam."

"Do not play the investigator looking for clues," Little Oak said, "this is not *What's My Line*. When the time comes, you will know the reading was correct."

Little Oak's rituals were not negotiable.

"Do not worry or fear; fear is confining. Crazy Horse never feared Custer. Your half of the message will find you."

As the sun added its own beauty to Ghost Dance Lake, Little Oak tied the canoe to the tree again and everyone headed back to Big Icicle. Zelda had plunged into the water so often that Eddie privately wondered if she could have been in the Navy in an earlier life.

"Water is the universal bond," Little Oak said, "stronger than super glue."

By the time the sun had risen the following morning, the citizens of Big Icicle had poked the coals in their heating systems and Little Oak had gone to a sacred place to spend her silent day. Harriet left a check for twice the advertised cost of the room and picked up a note left beside the coffee pot. It read, "I will see you one more time."

Going back to Tucson, everything but the scenery had changed. They talked less, pointed to fewer landmarks and counted fewer cattle. The ducks below Lewis and Clark Lake had only 30 minutes to show off.

How strange. A 90-pound relative of a world-famous Lakota Sioux Chief confesses that she only offends those who expect to be offended and never worries that her opinions might cost her a night's rent. How quaint. Big Icicle, a hub of simplicity; where you have to be yourself because there are so few opportunities to be anything else.

Harriet, aware that she would not see anything quite like this between Nebraska and Arizona, gladly exchanged her front seat for a chance to sleep in the back.

Zelda, still smarting from being left on the bank of Ghost Dance Lake, thought, *women are forever telling secrets*. But she had felt the strength and mystery of water and a kinship with Little Oak like the bonding that began when she slept on Eddie's lap for her first three nights in Arizona.

"Harriet should have arrested her," Zelda joked.

"Arrested who?" Eddie asked.

"The tree woman, Little Oak. Your wife could have charged her with attempted something or other and then brought her along to Tucson. The judge would have kept her overnight and then freed her with time served. She'd have a lot of new friends at the casinos."

To Eddie's delight, sameness was once again everywhere–the country was safe. They could speculate later about the power of three's and Little Oak's prophecy, "Let buffalo roam." Let textual hounds hunt for symbols in South Dakota's land of the shivering. Eddie abruptly ended this metaphysical foray when he missed his turn in Liberal, Kansas.

The air thinned and dried around Lordsburg, New Mexico. Three hours later, a green mileage sign read, "Tucson 23 miles." They unloaded the luggage and opened the main windows in the house in 30 minutes.

Gotcha!

Chapter 19

Over the years, Eddie Grace had had more than a hundred conversations with Rex Horne–some short, some long, all too long. When he and Zelda walked into the Wren a week after returning from their trip to Big Icicle, they found His Honor sitting alone and Eddie foolishly thought the next conversation might be different. Big mistake.

Hoping for a chance to explain his absence from the cafe, Eddie pulled up a chair next to the man famous for making people avoid him and began, "What've you been doing, Judge?"

"Nothing," Rex said flatly. "I have to do something about my socks. None of that crap they import from China ever feels right in my shoes."

"Sorry to hear that," Eddie said. "Maybe you need to get away for a while, take a trip. Harriet and I were just back to the Black Hills country. You ever been there?" One more big mistake.

"I've been all through that area," Rex said. "There's nothing out there but rocks on rocks and a bunch of Indians standing around waiting for Uncle Sammy to give them a new wigwam."

"Lord God," blurted a new customer as she scanned the heavens, "please consider re-creating that one."

Knowing it was time to look elsewhere for anyone interested

in his trip, Eddie excused himself and pulled up a chair next to Slack and Yancey. "So, what's happening?" he asked.

"You mean did we read the complete works of Plato while you were gone?" Sahara asked as she passed their table. "No we did not."

"It's funny, Ed," Yancey said looking up from his eggs-who-knows-what breakfast, "just yesterday we were sitting here saying how nice it would be if you stayed in South Dakota."

If it was painful finding out how little you were missed while you were on vacation, at least things were taking on a somewhat lighter tone.

"Damned good thing you didn't go to New York," Slack said. "They had 18 inches of snow last night. How are all those muggers going to get around?"

Still no call for anything about road conditions, weather or family in the Midwest.

A few minutes later, Yancey raised his hand for quiet, "Eddie, we missed you and Zelda so much that Sahara prepared a special program to celebrate your return. Take it away, Sahara."

"This little game," Sahara said, "is called, "How Celebrities Call Their Dogs"–a significant upgrade from the poetry Slack wanted to read."

"How's it go?" Eddie asked.

"I'll give you an easy example," Sahara said. "If a certain dog owner calls out to her dog, "Come on-a My House," whose dog is it?"

"Rosemary Clooney's," Eddie shouted and looked around to gauge the applause.

"Here here," Yancey said. "Now Sahara will give you four more clues to dog owners' names and for each correct answer, Gus will cover one lunch for you."

Sahara goes, "Number one, 'Damn the torpedoes! Full speed ahead!'"

Eddie guessed, "Harry Truman."

"Sorry, that was Admiral David Farragut."

"Number two, 'Approach.'"

Eddie went blank.

"That would be Judge Judy," Yancey said.

"Come up and see me sometime."

"Mae West," Eddie said. (He had seen all of her movies.)

"Last one," Sahara said. 'This way, Sinai, I don't have another forty years.'"

Eddie panicked, "Moses."

"Well kill the fatted calf," Yancey shouted. "Finally we can see how college improves your mind."

Eddie, suspecting all along that something was up, had planned a little game of his own.

"You want to hear about my dream last night?" he asked. The crowd followed that with a "yeah" that sounded more like an "oh, what the hell."

"I dreamed I was up on Woody Crook Trail, and something was wrong with the sky. Heaven seemed especially close."

"You were really dreaming," said a tourist from Spokane.

"And I was hugging this tall woman," Eddie said. "My right hand was on the small of her back."

"Ed," Yancey said, "you're supposed to hug the top one third."

A smart-looking guy from Colorado said, "If that's below the sixth vertebrae, you're a sex deviant."

"It wasn't my fault. I didn't know how tall she was."

Sahara asked if she was standing on a rock.

"Would you recognize her if you hugged her again?"

"Who cares if he hugs her again," Slack said. "What happened?"

"How old was she?" Gus asked.

"Maybe 60. Looked a little like a woman over on Ocotillo Street," Eddie said.

Zelda thought, *Guess where we're walking tomorrow*?

"Get on with it," Slack said, "I got an appointment with my gastro."

Now Eddie had them, "Then, my hand fell off."

82

"You mean your hand fell off the woman's back?"

"No, my hand fell off my arm. My dreams always have weird endings."

Yancey said, "Let me see if I heard you right. You're up on Woody Crook, with heaven above and a little of heaven below, and your hand falls off your arm?"

"Sorry," Eddie said.

"That's unforgivable," Yancey said. "Go back to South Dakota."

After a long glare, Sahara said, "Thanks for nothing, Eddie. By the way, the free lunches you just won in the dog-calling game don't start until 2022."

Cue Ball In The Corner Window

Chapter 20

A few weeks after Zelda had been home from the trip to Big Icicle and Ghost Dance Lake, she seemed to be a different dog—quieter, more sensitive to loud noises. Eddie thought she might have been examining her own destiny. They hadn't seen any ghosts at the lake and Harriet's arthritis didn't disappear when she splashed herself with its water. The lake was exceptionally clear but no one remembered seeing mysterious codes on the bottom that might account for the dog's changes.

Zelda didn't jump into an analysis of her new mood or announce the arrival of a new religion. She had no calling, no apparitions, no inspired text, and without these her chances of recruiting followers were like the Chicago Cubs' chances of getting to the World Series. Whatever feelings she had, they weren't like the one Eddie's father said he had when Ted Williams hit a homerun in his last at-bat in Boston.

So before she did a tell-all TV interview about the great mystery of Ghost Dance Lake and how she found her "time" in an inland body of fresh water, she waited for clarification the way Little Oak waited for communications from Sitting Bull.

Suspecting that Zelda's mood switch was rooted in the sharp drop-off from Little Oak's company to his own, Eddie suggested a short stop at Murphy's It's On The Table pool hall. This, he felt, would re-connect Zelda with down-to-earth people.

The horseshoe bar at Murphy's extended out toward the pool tables, giving Eddie and Zelda a chance to see and hear almost everything. None of the established pool sharks paused or looked up just because a man with a dog came in.

After ordering a coke, Eddie nudged Zelda and pointed to an aggressive player who was slamming pool balls around so hard that one ball actually flew off his table and onto the next.

"He reminds me of your friend, Rex," Zelda said.

Eddie added, "And have you noticed how the players chalk up and study the table before taking their shots?"

When Zelda didn't answer, Eddie called her attention to a well-dressed gentleman talking with the bartender.

"Notice, he has his personalized cue in a personalized case behind the bar."

"Does that mean he's the alpha male of the pool pack?" Zelda asked.

"Probably."

"And what's the point?"

"The point is success and recognition are universal drives that show up even in a pool hall. And those who win consistently earn a measure of admiration from those who have never, for example, run the table in a game of 8-ball."

"Yeah, well maybe we should have gone to a duckology institute where you would be properly appreciated." That sounded like the old Zelda.

Before Eddie could extend the idea of competition into nothingness, something very "non-pool" was developing that they could not ignore.

A 40-year old man in a bandana—also about 40 years old—claimed to have a moral question too complicated to allow a correct answer.

He began, "Suppose your mother asks you to rake the leaves in her front yard."

Several "Golden-Pool-Cue" winners standing nearby exchanged superior smiles, and one with a fractured sense of humor asked, "Would those leaves be green or brown?" No takers.

"Since Mother is big on promise-keeping and punctuality," the bandana man said, "you agree to do the work the next day. You start raking at 8 a.m. sharp, build up a quick sweat and whoa, you find a 50-dollar bill among the leaves. It couldn't have been dropped by somebody walking across the yard because Mother has a large 'keep-off' sign with the image of a smoking gun on it posted three feet from the sidewalk."

Eddie made a mental note.

The weathered man continued, "You wipe the sweat away and notice the wind is blowing steadily from a northeasterly direction. You decide the bill could have come from San Manuel but you're not going over there to read the lost and found. So, you keep the fifty and buy lunch for a woman you've been trying to meet for four years."

A customer with high principles hears this and says, "Should have contacted San Manuel law enforcement, no question."

"After two weeks, your mother asks if you saw anything unusual about the yard when you raked it. Now get this, she knows everything because she put the 50 bucks there to test your moral integrity."

"That's entrapment," said a man with three college credits in criminal law.

"You admit that you took the 50 bucks but insist that nothing was said about money found in the leaves."

Two of the original five listeners walked out.

"You insist that since there's no contract or even a handshake, a presumption of honesty in both parties and perhaps a finder's fee apply. You add that you have a right to deduct $37.50 from the lawn money for lunch with a beautiful woman–an expense you would not have incurred had you not believed that the money was yours. So, gentlemen, what's the answer?"

At this point, a delivery man paused with his dolly to suggest,

"Stop raking leaves and go dutch at lunch."

A second suggested that everybody pick a spot just northeast of Hearts Landing and get into a position to field 50-dollar bills.

"If I may," Zelda said to Eddie as they got up to leave, "next time we're here, treat these gentlemen to your explanation of why tennis balls bounce so much higher than strawberries."

"What are you talking about? I have never said a word about tennis balls and strawberries."

"I know," Zelda said, "but from my experience with you and your friends in Arizona, I think strawberries are next."

For Love Of Eileen

Chapter 21

For nearly half a century, Eileen O'Donnell was Tucson's favorite librarian. Her natural wit and allure tripled the number of male visitors to the reference section where she worked. She enjoyed a steady flow of both short and long-term relationships but she avoided matrimony, citing the risks of "wagering on the same horse every day." In a fishing phrase, Eileen preferred "catch and release."

For several years after her retirement, she had been staying at an assisted living facility near Hearts Landing. There, she retained her love of reading and kept in touch with several of Tucson's best writers; she also loved studying mirrors–with her in them.

Just as the spring flowers began to bloom, Eddie and Harriet took Zelda and an old Gibson guitar to see Eileen. The residents always welcomed a sing-along because that meant visitors who were willing to listen to their life stories and their predictions for the ever-shortening road ahead. Eddie had written a special song called "When The Moon Comes Over The Card Files" for the visit but Harriet wouldn't let him sing it.

Eileen greeted them all with hugs and introduced Zelda to new residents as the "babe" born in a South Dakota manger. Her high spirits notwithstanding, Eddie and Harriet could see that the "damned cancer" wasn't in remission.

Once these "upper classmen," as they called themselves, had made the journey from the dinner table to the lobby for dessert, Eileen coaxed Zelda into curling up at her feet.

"My all-time favorite love story," Eileen said to Harriet and Eddie, "has almost no plot and hardly any change in the characters—just a one-sided affair that got lost in the stacks." This was not new territory for the Graces, but they leaned forward to catch every detail again.

"For almost two years," Eileen continued, "a young man came in on his days off and sat where he could keep his mind off books; you see, he wasn't there to read Shakespeare or Faulkner for the meaning of life. On one of his stops, however, I saw him standing beside *Webster's Unabridged Dictionary*, open to the "L" section. No doubt he was looking up the difference between "love" and "lust" in order to learn what it was that he had. If I had been working in an oil stop in Fargo, this young romantic would have found the place."

Eileen's love story ended abruptly when a staff member unintentionally distracted her by collecting the dessert dishes. A moment later, she recalled the times she was voted sexiest librarian in Tucson and asked, "Do you think God will punish me for putting some of His handiwork on display?"

"Not a chance," Eddie answered immediately. "That's why He created mirrors and black dresses."

Zelda licked every hand in the place like they were all littermates. Eddie, meanwhile, distributed copies of such traditional favorites as "Red River Valley" and "Goodnight Irene" and urged everyone to sing. "The louder you sing the better I sound," he said.

For 20 minutes, they were the Arizona Senior Citizens' choir. No one talked about meds or wondered who would occupy their rooms when the flowers bloomed again.

When the evening ended, Eddie wanted to clear up any doubts that Eileen might have had about his musical talents. "I'm sorry," he said, "that one of my favorites, "I Can't Stop Loving You," didn't go so well."

Eileen knew he was looking for a denial and she would have none of it, "Oh, that's okay. I'm not so good in groups, either." Zelda whined a happy whine.

Three months later, when summer was in the Irish meadows, the soul of Eileen O'Donnell left Honeysuckle. She passed St. Patrick's Cathedral in New York City, circled once each over Killarney and Galway Bay and headed home.

On the day of the funeral, the Knights of Columbus sold beer for half price to anyone with a library card or an image of a shamrock. At Saint Cecelia's, three retired librarians from the area belted out or at, "When Irish Eyes Are Smiling." In his eulogy, Fr. Ragone said if times and circumstances had been different Saint Peter might have built his church on a "rock" in Dublin instead of Rome.

As expected, Eileen played the endgame the way she played life. She left her bank account to the parish and willed her personal items to friends. On the table beside her bed, they found an unsealed envelope addressed, "TO MY BOYFRIEND at the Library." The note inside said simply, "Come and see me."

Can The Pope Find Happiness In Dublin?

Chapter 22

When Eddie and Zelda arrived at the Wren a week after Mothers Day, Slack was complaining that the salmon he recently bought "tasted like a pelican had sat on it." Zelda looked Eddie's way and said softly, "Well, he'd be the one to know that." The rest of the lunch customers flinched at the comparison and Slack switched to the price of greeting cards.

"Have you noticed how expensive it's getting just to send a Mother's Day card?" he asked. "Why not write your own poem, like this? 'Roses are red, violets are blue. You're my mom, I love you.' There, less than half a buck for postage and she gets the message. Better still, grab a flower from your neighbor's rose bush and hand deliver both."

"I never thought I'd say this," Zelda said, "but I think Slack is right with his poem idea."

"I don't know," Eddie said. "Mothers deserve something that's more professional or looks like you took a few minutes to find just the right message. Something they can put on the piano maybe for others to see."

"They could see a home-made poem on the piano," Zelda said.

Eddie went on, "A classy card sends a stronger signal about love than a four-line poem, and you don't have to steal half of it the way Slack just did."

Zelda said, "Don't be so sure about this love stuff. Declarations of affection are like the polls in a close presidential election–both are within the margin of error."

Getting nowhere with his point about Mother's Day cards, Eddie was almost glad to see Slack moving toward his table.

"Hey Slacko," Sahara said, "did the Javelinas dump your trash can again? I heard you snarling over there."

"More snarling is what this country needs. With this cotton pickin' recession and the cost of food, Eddie here will have to get a smaller dog."

"Hear that, Big Time," Eddie said to Zelda, "shape up or I downsize."

"If the economy doesn't pick up soon," Slack said, "one of these days you're going to see a Mormon with just one wife."

Zelda thought, *But you won't see a drinking man skipping happy hour.*

"By the way Ed," Slack pushed another button, "you were at Eileen O'Donnell's funeral, right?"

"I was. Beautiful ceremony."

"I never cared much for her."

"Why's that?"

"I never knew what she was thinking."

Zelda thought, *At least she knew how to do it.*

"But what I wanted to ask you, Ed, is what did you think of Ragone's eulogy?"

"Fantastic!"

"That stuff about Peter building his church in Dublin doesn't bother you?"

Eddie said, "Not one bit."

Zelda grumbled silently, *Didn't this man ever go to class?*

"Well, I'm glad nothing bothers you, but damn it Eddie, I don't think the guy should talk like that. Some stuff should be left alone. Putting the Vatican in Ireland! What the hell would the Pope do in Ireland?"

"I don't know, Slack, but I think it would complement the overall mission of the papacy if the Pope sang "Danny Boy" now and then or visited a pub on Saint Patrick's Day."

"Well, speaking of craziness, did you hear about the little note that some smartass left on the holy water font the day of the funeral?"

Eddie had, and he wished he had put it there himself, but he waited for Slack's take on it.

"Well, there was only like a cup or so of holy water left in the font," Slack said, "so somebody left a note saying, 'Save the holy water for those who need it most.' That's probably a small sacrilege."

"I think it's pretty funny," Eddie said.

"Do me the kindness then of telling me why," Slack said.

"I think it's funny anytime somebody believes he knows how big the other guy's sins are. So, I found saving the holy water for the guy who's presumed to be worse off than the rest of us just a little amateurish."

"And I always thought you were a straight guy who liked things the way they are."

"I like routine around my house, but not necessarily around the holy water bowl."

"Just like a philosopher; you talk yourself into or out of everything. Next time you go into Saint Cecelia's, use all of the holy water."

Eddie and Zelda agreed never to ask Slack about same-sex marriage.

Deregulated Long Before Reagan

Chapter 23

Much of what happens in Embers, Arizona, (the town where Eddie and Harriet lived before retiring in Hearts Landing) is unintentional, random, something added to the moment. Things aren't planned the way they are in Iowa and Minneapolis. The future of copper mining in Embers pretty much left in the 70's, leaving what remained to go either up or down on its own. These days, the financial sector is wherever the man with 300 dollars in his pocket happens to be. Macro-managers and licensed planners of planning haven't caught on the way mining once did.

Nevertheless, Embers is a joyful center for creativity; a refreshing hub of rainbows and poetry. A California-owned-and-operated café offers a "25% discount for all children 70 and under." Lifestyles in Embers rarely follow anything popularized by corporate investments or political correctness. On every block, "create" trumps "copy."

Suppose for a moment that a certain laid-back dude in Embers is walking in the general direction of downtown one morning and the soles of his shoes are wearing painfully thin. He knows a shoe repair shop just off Grayson Park where the owner might swap a pair of cheap soles for a couple of saxophone lessons. Having completed the deal, the dude, now sporting cheap-but-improved soles, meets a man leaving for Pueblo, Colorado. He gets into the man's car and they drive to Lordsburg, New Mexico, where the passenger meets a woman who offers him a place to hang out for half of the unspecified rent. Four years later, after stops in Saint Paul and Seattle, the man with the discounted soles is back in the former mining town. Unrestrained impulse is just one of Embers' many charms.

Life in Embers is not driven into a corner. It is let loose, to grow, to explode, to amuse, sometimes to offend. Whatever its purpose or meaning, living comes with happenings, not with schedules. It turns more on chance and love of the moment than on designs and blueprints. Deregulated long before Ronald Reagan made the word popular, the city is a cultural pay station, with instinct and nature locked in and time locked out. Travelers to this small town need not notify friends or acquaintances of either their arrival or their departure times. Like lovers, the residents of Embers find their way without a clock.

As usual, Eddie drove the 80-mile trip from Hearts Landing to Embers just under what the speed signs dictated while Harriet tapped her foot and raised the possibility of being rear-ended by a golf cart. She read speed limits aloud, announced miles covered per hour, bemoaned time wasted and computed all of that into personal dissatisfaction.

On the outskirts of Embers, Eddie crossed an intersection just as the yellow light changed to red and he saw some humor in that, "You see, Harriet, if I hadn't driven exactly as I did, we wouldn't have made that light."

Harriet asked herself, *why does a man committed to correct thinking sell his life for such trivia?* Eddie's driving was that custom-equals-comfort thing again. He also counted on her to accept his comment as amusement, intended to minimize the suffering of a husband and wife in the same car for two hours.

The Graces had found their way to Embers over three decades before Zelda's arrival when he needed a job and the local branch college needed a humanities teacher. They arrived with 32 cents

95

in their bank account and hoped they wouldn't need a root canal before Eddie got his first paycheck. The tiny house they rented for $90 a month had one wall heater and no insulation to keep them either warm or cool. Entertainment for the first month consisted of the Saturday night auction on Main Street and quarts of Lucky Lager beer. On this return visit, they parked in a vacant lot downtown (a mile above sea level) and lugged themselves up the 57 public steps to Shinny's Shanties.

Joe Shinauer, Grandfather of the current operator, opened the bed and breakfast in the early twentieth century and later popularized it with tales of his personal adventures. In his favorite story, the old man told of his arrest in 1908 for streaking in front of the horse that the Mayor's wife was riding in the annual Miner's Day parade. The following morning, the judge fined him 50 dollars–10 for startling the Mayor's wife and 40 for spooking the horse. The "injured party," the wife, never filed a complaint. Joe's only regret was that Main Street wasn't wider. Touched-up tales of Joe's streak and similar alleged events made the Shanties the place to sleep in Embers.

The streets in this haven for artists are irregular, chunky and just wide enough for a fat man to pass a bicycle. For safety reasons, visitors are advised to look down as often as they look up.

At sundown, Harriet, Eddie and Zelda walked carefully down to the Hallucination Bar, famous for a biblical cocktail called The Fall. Zelda was one of very few dogs on a leash; the others moved around exhibiting a dominion that comes with the unregulated life.

Since the Graces wanted to look and listen in Embers, they chose a table where they could see patrons coming in, catch the eye of the bartender and overhear samples of small town wit and whimsy.

From the bar....

"You're a little early tonight, aren't you, Blanche?"

"I'm a little gloomy too, so light up the night."

From a customer passing the Grace's table ....

"Don't I know you?"

"I don't think so," Eddie answered, "we haven't been here in eight years."

"Of course, it was in another life."

Above the bar a life-size nude watched over a mixture of singles, doubles and partials and of course, the usual smattering of "normally strange" tourists. At least twice, a patron temporarily changed places with the bartender and nobody missed a drink.

"Good looking dog you got there, Old Man," a fellow in a raincoat said. "Is she your way of making friends?"

"No, why?" Eddie asked.

"When I majored in Early Armenian Mindsets, my mentor said a man hangs out with a dog because his soul lacks growth potential, know what I'm saying?"

Harriet hoped Zelda would take a hunk out of the man's calf but she chose instead to feed him, "Will you be writing your doctoral dissertation on soul growth?" To which the man replied, "Haven't decided. I have six proposals on the backseat of the car I'm driving. Say Man, if you want to do a seminar in LA I have contacts up and down Sunset Boulevard."

Harriet pointed to two men discussing the sale of a coat. The man with the coat—on his back—handed it to the potential buyer, who then admired himself in the mirror below the nude. As the customer gave the owner a down payment for the coat, the seller said, "I'm probably going to get married next week, so I'll have to borrow it back for that." When the piano player went on break at nine, Harriet suggested they head back to their shanty.

"I don't suppose any of that impressed you, did it?" Eddie asked Zelda after they had cleared the Hallucination crowd.

"Actually," she said, "it was great seeing people whose second question was not 'how did you meet your wife?'"

Just then, a middle-aged man in a "Lost Tribes of Woodstock" T-shirt shouted, "Last performance of *The Embers Embrace*. Just follow the arrows to The Luxury Playhouse on Stella Avenue. Hurry, hurry, hurry."

Shadows & Cash

Chapter 24

It doesn't take long for tourists to get to the end of a street in Embers. Either the street becomes impassable or their curiosity runs low. After eight minutes of obeying chalk arrows and assorted signs, Eddie and Harriet stood in the backyard of an isolated frame house with a large second-floor window and "Luxury Playhouse" printed on the back door (same chalk, it appeared). No valet parking, no complimentary champagne, and "standing room only" meant the Luxury provided no seats. But a theatrical performance in a secluded part of a secluded town signaled entrepreneurship not found everywhere, so they joined the nine theatre-goers and two neighborhood dogs waiting for the opening scene.

A rough sketch of Rodin's *The Kiss* dangled from the second floor balcony. Below it stood an empty 32-ounce Mellow Sip coffee can. To the can's right, a felt-tip warning read, "Over 60? Don't watch more than two performances in 36 hours; your tonsils will grow back."

"Don't believe it," Hector, the fellow standing next to Eddie said. "This is my third night of double features this week."

"I was thinking of leaving tomorrow," Eddie said, "but now I…"

"Eddie," Harriet stopped him, "we're leaving tomorrow."

A blue light bulb in the upstairs window flashed and the producer/director/greeter stood on the balcony reminding the audience that the actors were "working their way up" and not to forget the Mellow Sip can.

"And now," he said, "*The Embers Embrace*."

As a tenor sax man played "Embraceable You," a light-weight shade in the large window dropped, revealing the "low-definition" outline of two lovers seated on a slow-turning coffee table.

A white-haired lady in the back crossed herself and whispered, "Saints in Heaven, save us."

"I've got pictures from last night if you want to see them," Hector said to Eddie.

An 80-ish woman in the front row—polar opposite of the white-haired lady—said to her friend, "I'm auditioning for tomorrow's performance."

"At your age?"

"Yes at my age, and I've got a boyfriend too who's not on a respirator."

Harriet, her investigator's instincts alert, spotted a fellow who looked like retired law enforcement and asked him quietly, "Have the cops checked this place out?"

"Can't say." he answered. "It's hard to bring charges against people inside their own homes, with the shades drawn (he smiled broadly) and one bulb for light."

Zelda thought, *Who says perception isn't everything?*

On the coffee table, the performers varied their alignments according to comfort and the fans' responses. What sounds they made were muffled by the "orchestra." And like journalists at a presidential press conference, both males and females in the audience guarded their front-row spaces.

The 80-year old boasted to her friend, "There are so many things in life that I want to do."

With that, the first half of the show ended and the director appeared at the window.

"First," he said, "please note that during the entire first act nobody took off any clothing (laughter). And for the second act, we will actually be adding clothing."

"Bummer," shouted an anonymous first-time attendee.

"Second, I've been watching some of you. Your eyes are going to hell fast if you don't blink. Of course you're all welcome to stay as long as you like–or as long as you can see–but remember, our insurance doesn't cover those over 60 who watch for more than 16 minutes. And finally, make a note on your calendar, next week's production is the ever-sizzling, *Cat On A Hot Sin Roof*."

The performers in the second act understood how imagination can overwhelm an audience; they also understood special effects and the importance of the Mellow Sip can. In other words, the blinking problem in the audience was going to continue.

The additional clothing that the director promised was a New York Yankees baseball cap for the leading man and Prada for his lady.

"Honest to God, Eddie," Harriet said, "is this the look-and-listen part we talked about?"

Harriet stepped away for some brief bending exercises just as the actress did her signature slither across the table.

"Ooooh, she could get a sliver doing that," said the front-row woman with "so many things" to do

For their last scene, the "musical director" chose "We've Only Just Begun."

That evening, the Luxury Playhouse owed nothing to the ancients. There was no beginning-middle-and-end stuff. No masks, no exposition–in the usual sense–and not a single utterance of the "F" word–just a story and lots of imagination both on and off the stage. Since the action didn't rise much, it didn't fall much. For stage craft, a rope contraption by which the choreographer in the wings kept the coffee table moving.

A man who came in late said he had four years of high school acting if they needed an understudy.

Then after only six minutes of the best moves south of Phoenix, the couple broke their embrace and it was over. No curtain calls. Just people with art for sale and looking for lunch tomorrow. The play and the coffee can were the "things." As always, Embers did not run on regular time. Life came and went in unexpected bits and pieces.

Leaving the Luxury, a woman called the performance "historically hysterical," and said she hadn't felt such "heightened awareness" since the Sixties. As she dropped her tip into the coffee can, she also dropped her phone number. Turning to her companion, she said, "If I don't get a call, next week I'm putting my number on the back of a picture of me at a Hollywood audition fifty years ago and I'm throwing that in there."

The three weary travelers dragged their "newly-aware" bodies back up the steps to slumber a world away from Tucson.

After seven hours of intermittent sleep, Harriet was anxious to get going. She paid the bill, grabbed complementary coffee for two and hurried everybody down the stairs where she thanked God for letting them beat the bed and breakfast to the bottom of the mountain.

Unable to quench her natural curiosity for the "dirt," Zelda scanned the entire downtown area for the stars of *The Embers Embrace*. No actors or directors around; not even anyone who looked like he might not have blinked in a while.

The only recognizable leftover from the evening before was the fellow in the Hallucination Bar who bought the coat that he would have to lend back to the previous owner. He was explaining his "reality" to three tourists and a cat that he called, First and Second Corinthians.

Harriet was already dozing in the back seat as they passed Saint Bridgett's Church on the way home. Zelda admired the architecture, flashed back momentarily to the Luxury Playhouse and needled Eddie, "I see your eyes have settled back into your head very nicely."

36 Ways To Say "I Hate You"

Chapter 25

Zelda's mystery bloodline prohibited her from competing in licensed dog shows. Eddie regretted this, but he knew it wouldn't pay to go back to Big Icicle to get more on her ancestry.

Ribbons and trophies aside, Eddie took Zelda to Tucson's annual all-breed competition in part to confirm his confidence in her beauty and temperament. The temperature stayed in the low 70's that Saturday, keeping sweat and sunburn at a minimum

Before they reached the show rings, Eddie stopped to talk to a man sitting beside a small travel trailer with, "Great Danes Forever" in big orange letters on both sides.

"That's the funniest looking Great Dane I've ever seen," he said looking at Zelda. "I like her one ear there, sort of tipped forward. Can she move it up and down?"

"Maybe she can," Eddie said, "but I've never seen her do anything but wiggle it when her food arrives."

Zelda thought, *I hate being talked about when I'm present.*

"My father-in-law had an ear something like that," the Dane owner said. "He could move it up just a bit. In the "up" position, it acted like an antenna. He could hear everybody in the county."

"Wow!" Eddie said.

"My wife didn't inherit his ear. She hasn't heard a thing I've said in 28 years."

"You must be exaggerating."

"By the way, I'm Oscar, proud owner of AKC Champion, Ingrid, there," the man said as he pointed to a Dane bitch stretched out beside her crate.

"I'm Eddie and this is Zelda. We came early so we could talk to some dog people."

"You just hit gold, Buddy. Know why I'm so far away from the action? Too many handlers have their damned rock music up so loud you can hear it in Kansas. Uh, be careful where you're stepping there; that stuff is hell to get off your shoes."

Eddie checked to see if it was too late.

"Some platinum billionaire is always yelping like he just busted an ankle. We're a long way from "Some Enchanted Evening." You like music?"

"Yes, especially smooth saxophone stuff–Stan Getz."

"Another thing, my old Thesaurus gives 36 words or phrases that mean "hate," and that list doesn't include "pissed off.""

"I'm not sure I follow," Eddie said.

"Well look right into the eyes of the dog handlers and owners here today and you will see every one of those synonyms for hate–envy, venom, rancor, jealousy and maybe some death threats. It's a blood sport man, and I'm not talking blood in a pedigree. Dog shows are 'get the other guy's dream and stomp on it!'"

Even in Tucson's city parks, good grass is almost as hard to find as water buffalo. A young girl, nine or so, ran into a grass problem as she waited for her Old English Sheepdog to do his bathroom duty in the barren area near her show ring. "Mother," she said, "Gaylord doesn't like to go on the dirt."

At times it was hard to tell who was showing off–the dogs or the judges. At dog shows, everyone expects the animals to strut their stuff, but the bright wearing apparel and imperial bearing of the judges made them look like the Vatican Swiss Guard. The eyes of owners and handlers alike were on them as they stepped smartly from animal to animal.

Maneuvering around small exercise pens, grooming tables and event staff, Eddie and Zelda paused occasionally to hear what else dog people talk about during the excitement of American Kennel Club competition.

"But Elizabeth," an overdressed woman asked her friend at one of the soft drink stands, "can't you re-schedule so you can stay for the reverend's talk tomorrow?"

"I would but I've missed one Phoenix meeting already this year."

"We could sit near the back and you could slip out a little early."

"Oh, okay. I'll stay for 10 minutes, but then I've got to move my ass."

Zelda took notice of an Airedale Terrier, especially its alertness and showy body language. She was even more focused on the owner who was washing her hair in what appeared to be the dog's water bucket, but by then she had seen enough and didn't comment.

As Eddie and Zelda watched the maze of breeds and groups, the popular opinion that dog shows are canine competition in name only was heavily underscored. Scrambling for ribbons and the judge's favor was a fair price for points from AKC.

But Eddie put all negatives aside for the pleasure of watching well-schooled animals gliding effortlessly around each ring and for the amusement provided by passionate and "hate-filled" dog lovers.

Not far from the Toy Group, Zelda made eye contact with a five-pound Long Coat Chihuahua that the handler was busily encouraging for the Best-Of-Breed competition. Because Zelda said he was "so cute," Eddie bent down to the dog and asked, "How you doing, little fella?" The handler, with venom aplenty, snapped, "I beg your pardon, this dog does not answer to 'little fella.' His name is General Santiago–and don't distract him when he's getting ready to poop!"

Zelda and Eddie privately evaluated dogs that were wooly or

slick, noisy or quiet and a few that were fatter than Roman tax collectors. Zelda introduced herself to one magnificent Irish Setter and let him know that she, Zelda, had never lost a dog event in her life. That was correct because she had never been entered in a dog event. She'd picked up her fondness for selected disclosure from her friends at the Wren.

Eddie's amusement went sky high later as he and Zelda watched a middle-aged couple pack their cab-over camper for the drive back to California. Apparently in appreciation for the awards that a portly Basset Hound named "Claude" had received, the husband watched proudly as his "boy" worked over a large bowl of chocolate chip ice cream. The woman stopped loading gear long enough to wave Zelda and Eddie closer.

"Want something for your memory book?" she asked.

"Of course," Eddie responded.

"You see," the woman explained, "Claude will eat only one kind of ice cream–dark chocolate chip."

Zelda thought, *I gotta listen to this woman.*

"Notice how purposeful and efficient he is," she said.

"He pushes the ice cream around very deliberately," Eddie added. "And he seems to be nosing the chips to the side of the bowl."

"Right. Look now, he's finished," said the wife.

Eddie did, and added, "But he hasn't finished the chocolate chips."

"You got it," the wife said with a purple-ribbon grin, "he always saves the chips for my husband."

Two-Finger Dip And Rub

Chapter 26

"Do you know what it's like when a sister-in-law arrives and never says how long she's staying?" Eddie asked Zelda. "It's like an undated death threat; each morning you think this is the day she says she's staying permanently."

"Give Lilac time to work that out. She just got here three days ago," Zelda said.

"Lilac is a clothes-shedding, custom-trashing leftover from the Sixties who never gives a hint about what she might do next."

"You've got a bias against liberated women," Zelda said.

"Well, Lilac is too old to be running around my house in outfits that fit sixth graders."

"Any other kind takes half of the fun out of life, Cowboy. Before you die, you should try to become something other than behind the times."

"Get in the car," Eddie said, "I'm going over to ask Gus if he needs a greeter at the Wren."

"I'll sell you some time on the glider," Zelda offered. "No payments until 2015."

"I think she's already measured the room," Eddie said.

"Once again you're bleeding all over a non-story. When did you last see Lilac?" Zelda asked.

"Almost four years ago."

"So she's sixty-three now, and single. Relax, she won't be interested in Hearts Landing for another 20 years."

At the Wren, Eddie got right to the point, "I need answers fast."

Slack, who had heard of Lilac's arrival, said. "You came to the right place, Buddy. If you had given her some cheap flowers at the airport, you could have said how you hoped they wouldn't die before she had to go home."

Sahara took a seat that she hoped would block any more coaching from the Oklahoma truck driver.

"Everybody here knows I'm a home-and-castle kind of guy," Eddie said. "Nothing kinky inside my property lines. I expect only a few things from other people and one of them is if you're sixty years old, act like it."

Sahara looked worried. She didn't think Eddie would notice if Harriet repainted their bedroom.

"So the second night Lilac is here," Eddie said, "she goes to her room real early. (Two customers turned his way.) Not a sound from her for an hour. So Harriet, aware that Lilac's health had slipped some, asked me to check on her. I tapped lightly on her door and asked if she was okay."

Two more customers turned.

"She said, 'just a second, let me look. . . Oh yes sir, I'm very okay.' Then she opens the door just a crack to confirm her total disregard for all decency and whispers, 'Not tonight, Big Guy.' She's coming on to me, I can feel it."

"I hear you, Buddy," Slack said.

Sahara smiled broadly to accompany two tables of giggles and said, "Eddie dearest, the imagination is always the last thing to go."

"You didn't see the look in her eyes," Eddie said as he re-lived the moment.

Zelda slid closer to Eddie and mumbled, "You weren't looking at her eyes, were you?"

"She probably likes the feeling of dry Arizona air," Sahara said.

"You're right," Eddie said, "in every pore."

"They must be advertising a patch on TV for whatever you've got, Ed," Gus said.

"You could have told us, Ed," Yancey said with a grin, "we're here for you."

"Listen, the next morning I come out of the bedroom and there she was on her way to the bathroom."

"Pores open?" Sahara asked.

"Let's just say she was shower ready."

A customer wanted to know if Lilac was wearing a towel.

"Hell no," Eddie said, "all she was wearing was one of those bracelets that are supposed to keep you from falling over! I could have used one myself."

"Did you warn Harriet about the Lilac threat?" Sahara asked, sensing more fun on the way.

"Sure, right after breakfast today."

"And what did she say?"

"She said, 'My dear man, you're eating too much candy.'"

Slack said he didn't want to offend Harriet but, "Since J. Edgar Hoover died, a lot of FBI agents can't tell the difference between an invitation to romance and a declaration of war."

Gus pointed to a small bruise on Eddie's forearm and said, "Be sure she sees that and then tell her the doctor was pretty sure it wasn't contagious."

"But I hate to tell a lie," Eddie said.

"Ed," Gus came back. "don't you know that lies work better than truth three quarters of the time?"

After some scattered applause, Yancey closed, "Having reached a level of understanding commensurate with the needs of all parties, let us await further inspiration–or in the case of Eddie v. Lilac, further exposure."

• • •

Lilac had heard so much about the café where Eddie and Zelda "met the world" that she persuaded Harriet to take her there for coffee the following morning. Harriet did, but only with Lilac's promise not to talk to anyone except Sahara.

"I doubled my time with my shrink three months ago," Lilac said as Harriet led her to a small table well apart from any customers.

"Good," Harriet said, "what did she suggest?"

"She didn't suggest anything that I could believe. She asked me 'how did that make me feel' six or eight times every session and then talked for 30 minutes about her damned rhubarb. She doesn't know any more about my inner self than a bulldog knows about Easter."

"Did you bring up the clothes thing?"

"I did, and she asked if I thought my fascination with nudity showed a desire to return to the Garden of Eden, and if that was why I changed my name to Lilac."

"Eddie," Harriet said, "should take up counseling. He's a good listener."

"When I was 20," Lilac said, "I took my clothes off because I looked great."

"You always look great, Sis."

"Now I take them off and look in the mirror to see what needs to be painted over, rubbed out, pushed up or strapped in."

"I understand that better than the Garden of Eden connection."

"Forty years ago," Lilac said, "I thought clothes were just another useful gimmick in the free market model. You know, tell women that the right threads will get them an NFL quarterback and they'll buy every time."

Harriet thought, *Forty years ago, you were lost without a map, and you had a very expensive philosophy called "Get It Now."*

"You ever see those look-thirty-again lotions they advertise on TV?" Lilac asked.

"There are twenty every day, so yes, I have."

"Well, I got a case of that stuff. Actually, a boyfriend who was trying to tell me something paid for it. So every day for six months, I scoop up some of that stuff with my middle and index fingers and smear it around. Same routine every day–two-finger dip and rub, dip and rub, and I wait for the aging process to reverse itself."

"Did it work?" Harriet asked without thinking.

"Does it look like it worked? If it had worked, those two fingers would be about 12 years old now."

"It's hard to go back, Sis," was the best Harriet had. "But how are you doing now?"

"I'm looking for a relationship, what else? Close, like the one you and Eddie and Zelda have."

Harriet said the bonding started when Zelda was young and she slept next to their bed.

Lilac said she'd settle for somebody who'd sleep anywhere in the house.

"Imagine that," she went on, "a guy and a dog so close that they look like they're talking to each other and I can't get a man without a car to hang out for more than 48 hours."

"He's so proud of that dog," Harriet said to change the subject. "He won't show it publicly very often but whenever somebody asks about her, he carries on like he's being interviewed by a syndicated columnist."

"I would have liked your friend Eileen O'Donnell at the library. She must have had more boyfriends than the place had books."

"And she understood the boyfriends," Harriet said.

Gus personally replaced their ice tea glasses so he could look more closely at the woman who was doing most of the listening but he couldn't place her.

"I spent my youth and three marriages searching for myself," Lilac said. "I moved 14 times, from one Buckingham Palace to another–trailer parks. Somehow, I always missed myself."

Lilac respected but never imitated an orderly life such as Eddie's and Harriet's. She never got up at the same time more than three mornings in a row. She admired Eddie's attachment to writers who shook the world and forced the English language into some measure of accuracy. She said he would look right at home sitting on a sack of potatoes in a busy grocery store, reading *The Rise and Fall of The Roman Empire*. But it was Eddie's self-deprecating humor, not his academic background that amused her most. "It's not that I'm incompetent," she remembered him saying. "It's just that I can't do anything."

Conceding that Eddie was "incompetent" and might be perceived as a good fit with a sack of potatoes, Harriet nevertheless assured Lilac that he was neither a domestic liability nor a public nuisance, and that she had never considered trading up.

Hoping that some good would come from the get together, Harriet asked, "So where did your current psychiatrist go to school?" Lilac's answer offered no hope, "Hell, I don't know. She's got certificates all over the walls. One says, "Your New Life Begins At Moose Jaw" something or other; I should grab a couple of those phony diplomas sometime for my bird cage."

As Lilac packed her things the next morning, Eddie made a point of saying how beautiful the Delta must be, and how hard it is these days to find places like that. Privately, he believed the best place for Lilac that day was in a seat on a non-stop flight to Dixie.

Driving home from the airport, Eddie said to himself, "Dear God, don't let that woman away from the Deep South. I'll never ask for anything again. I'll obey every commandment, and if there are any new ones, I'll obey them too without even looking them over."

Before Lilac's flight had passed El Paso, Harriet had restored order in the guest bedroom. As expected, she found a small box with a piece of Mata Ortiz pottery inside. The attached note read, "I think this will fit nicely with the rest of the artwork in your living room, Harriet. Since I wasn't able to find just the right gift for Eddie, I have decided to send him a framed photo of me at the beach several summers ago. I'm sitting on the hood of an antique Volvo. I have titled it, "Original Condition." It's guaranteed to lighten the mood in his study. Lilac"

The Pre-cemeterians' Social

Chapter 27

Eddie knew he was getting older when the Get-On-A-Roll motorized chair company began sending brochures that promised mobility, independence and a "free book of fiber-rich dessert recipes with each scooter purchased." He sensed it when his dermatologist kept burning off "maturity spots" and the annual flu shot left a 10-hour sting in his left shoulder.

For Eddie, the golden age of crew cuts and pink shirts had come and gone without so much as a public service announcement to that effect. He understood that time has a way of dropping in on life and that if you hang around long enough you no longer make a difference. He accepted these truisms and avoided boring others with talk about the rights of senior citizens. Like aging actresses, Zelda and Harriet also recognized the need to exchange some of their youthful vigor for a piece of mid-life reality.

With those compromises and the mellowing process in place, Harriet proposed a party for Zelda's fifth birthday. She reluctantly invited Slack after Eddie assured her that the plainsman had promised not to ask anyone to play pin something somewhere. The Graces didn't bother to run up the five-o'clock-meeting flag after Sahara offered to manage the bar. They received only one rather formal regret, which Eddie read aloud first thing at the

113

get together, "We are so sorry that we will not be attending your birthday party, Zelda. Our health is not what it was five years ago. Sincerely, the Bushes and Shrubs, former residents of your backyard."

Sahara then announced, "We have gin, bourbon, wine coolers, one bottle of Goats Do Roam, and a jug of something that will keep any goat from ever roaming again. If none of that sounds good, we have red licorice."

Harriet had spread out chicken wings, cheeses, a mound of vegetables, and some special hot sauce from Nogales. When everyone had tested each, Yancey raised a glass of red wine and wished Zelda "long life and happiness, if that's possible with Eddie."

A neighbor with "Joe" on his company shirt said how Zelda always seemed to know exactly what Eddie was saying.

"Humm," Eddie said, "she never heard anything I said about our defenseless shrubbery."

A second guest, with "Zelda for President" on her T-shirt, called Zelda "the smartest dog west of Memphis."

"Well she should be," Rex said, "Ed here could have learned the Spanish language in the time he's spent with that dog."

Slack said he could see the love in Zelda's eyes every time she looked at him. Harriet told him that was the food look, not the love look.

Eddie bragged how soon Zelda learned how to catch a Frisbee and how to operate those senior-friendly doorknobs in the house.

"Are all the dogs in South Dakota that smart, Eddie?" Slack asked. "In Oklahoma, we always said things up north were pretty slow."

Without any motivation, Rex then tried to explain the future of female thumbs. He said the thumbs of TV newswomen were curving backward so fast that in five or six generations their thumbs would circle back to touch their wrists. These thumbs, he said, would be useless, like ear lobes, but they would survive because the thrust of evolution is partly controlled by power and opportunity—both of which TV women now enjoy.

The Grace's next-door neighbor re-loaded on the Goats Do Roam and said, "Rex, could you hold that story for Zelda's 40th birthday?"

Harriet pointed to a sign on the patio that read, "Your first 30 seconds of nonsense is free; after that, we cannot guarantee your safety."

Yancey said, "Rex, be sure to let us know what the National Academy of Sciences says about the emergence of circular thumbs in females."

Joe in the union shirt didn't understand how money and success could make straight thumbs "do a circle."

Sahara, being one whose thumbs were still pretty straight, said, "Listen Your Honor, instead of making certain that you will never again be allowed inside Eddie's house, why don't you save this for a science fiction novel?"

"Simple, and a basic of Capitalism that you've obviously missed," Rex said. "You see, I can't get a book published until I get noticed by a publisher and I can't get noticed by a publisher until I get a book published."

"God, I will never learn," Sahara muttered.

Zelda offered her take to Eddie, "Now is the perfect time to say there's a lot to be said for saying nothing."

As a way of keeping Rex quiet, Slack gave the gist of why he never intended to set another date for cleaning his house. "If on Tuesday," he said, "I make a plan to clean on Sunday, you know what that does? That shoots every day between Tuesday and Sunday because I'm thinking about the misery of dusting and looking for juice spots on the counter tops–and life is hell all week because I planned more than two minutes ahead."

This worked better than expected. Rex remembered that he had signed up for a food IQ test in the morning and that the sponsors were serving a free gourmet breakfast for those who participated in the research.

Forgetting Harriet's earlier warning, Slack renewed his offer to teach Sahara the Panhandle Four Step, a dance allegedly named for the distance between the bar and the bedroom in his flatland cabin.

"Slack," Yancey asked, "why do you keep making passes at Sahara?"

Sahara answered for him, "He's hoarding rejections."

As Harriet said good night to Joe in the company shirt, she asked, "Do you think there's a future for looped thumbs?"

Joe answered, "It'll never happen–but then that's what they said about Monday Night Football."

Could Have Been Worse

Chapter 28

Two months after Zelda's birthday party, Rex, the judge, died in his sleep. There were questions about the cause of death but since those who knew him were trying harder to forget him than to remember him, nobody pushed for anything more than a routine investigation by the four-officer Hearts Landing police department. Various other inconsequential matters came and went quickly and the judge was laid to rest with his wildflower questions, his theory of women's thumbs and his eye-witness accounts of non-events. The family denied a request, Rex's, that selected passages from a biography of Alexander the Great be read at the funeral.

Two weeks later, Eddie, Yancey and Slack arranged a short memorial service at the café. Gus called this trio, "The Society for the Preservation of Rex Horne in His Current State." Sahara had the day off but agreed to stop by after the medical examiner assured her that the body was Rex's.

The demands of truth made the memorial liturgy awkward. When three people sang "How Great Thou Art," Yancey said it was confusing, ill-advised, and "scandalous if not worse." Rex's next door neighbor said the Judge had died from an overdose of himself. Feelings were mixed about where, that is in which di-

117

rection, if any, his soul went. Gus said he had always thought of heaven as a huge Yellowstone-like place, and he hoped that God had prepared a section somewhere on the perimeter especially for Rex and the hard of hearing.

Several attendees, all strangers, offered short eulogies ranging from "river-water" salvation to "we all have to go sometime." One of them said how sad it is when death comes without warning and friends of the dearly departed don't have a chance to say good-bye. Another said how everyone would miss Rex, but the group understood the word "miss" to mean that they would know Rex wasn't around rather than their lives would be empty without him.

When Slack had an opportunity, he said, "Damn it, I warned Rex that he needed to do something good for somebody pretty soon or when his funeral came along, what the hell were we going to say?"

Zelda, leaving no doubt about what she intended to say, whispered to Eddie, "It could have been worse; he could have lived another 30 years."

As always, Eddie sought safety in the middle, saying he wished Rex had had a few more years to expand his circle of friends. Sahara said to another waitress that it was too bad that he couldn't have done this a long time ago.

The highlight of the service came when a female soloist did a couple of anti-dance steps to the old favorite, "When The Saints Go Marching In." Her improvised rendition took her gliding from table to table and ended with a plaintive howl that was only a decibel or two shy of raising Rex.

At last, Yancey held up a plain white envelope from Agnes, Rex's ex-wife, who had always believed in the afterlife. Yancey removed the short note inside, and read it to the group, "I spent three very long years married to this man. He wasn't a bad person, really, but no matter how hard I tried, we just couldn't get along. Good luck, God."

And A Cartridge In A Pear Tree

Chapter 29

Yancey's health issues kept him from actively participating in some social events, but when Sahara invited him to go with her to the Free Country Dog Run on Christmas morning, he forgot all about his arthritic knee. *Who knows*, he thought, *a tall raven-haired beauty at my side, a piece of fake Mediterranean jewelry stuck on my best hat and I could be taken for the long-overdue Fourth King of Orient.*

The place wasn't crowded. A collection of undistinguished dogs had just finished a 30-yard race, with a tiny Italian Greyhound winning by three lengths and the Saint Bernard conceding after a 10-yard wobble.

"So, Mr. Nebraska, what did you do for Christmas when you were a kid?" Sahara asked.

"Well, the very first thing we did in the morning was check all of our parts to see if anything was frozen," Yancey said. "The wind blows cold on the prairie, Christmas or not."

Sahara flinched.

"Then we counted the livestock and my father checked to see if the Chevy would start before we got all dressed up for church and couldn't get there."

An established "hip reader" nearby saw Sahara and hoped

that Yancey was her grandfather. Oblivious to the noisy kids and dogs, the young man memorized each anatomical marker between Sahara's boots and the Santa Clause cap on her head.

Having encountered fever machines before, Sahara took Yancey's arm, passed within two steps of her admirer and said in a soft southern drawl, "We can take that up again when we get to Vegas, Senator."

A minute later, Sahara asked, "Has he blinked yet?"

Glancing back, Yancey could see the fellow drinking from the fountain. *Ice cold water,* he thought, *just what a man in his condition needs, even in December.*"

"Did you read the paper this morning?" Sahara asked.

"I forgot. Must have been too busy picking out something to wear to Vegas," Yancey answered.

"Another guy was shot and killed last night on Tucson's east side," Sahara said, "and you know what it was about?"

"A parking place?"

"Probably dumber than that; it was over a trash can."

"If a coyote eyeballs my Schnauzer," Yancey said, "I just throw a rock at him and he starts thinking of a different place to hunt. If that dude doing the shooting last night had had a slingshot instead of a gun, who knows, those two guys might be watching a high school basketball game together next week."

Eddie and Zelda had walked into the area without attracting much attention. They exchanged holiday greetings with several dog people before doing the same with Yancey and Sahara. When a stranger cupped Zelda's head in her hands and said how loving she seemed, Yancey–with the shooting still on his mind–turned to her and asked, "Do you think holding a kid like that for a few minutes every day would keep him out of trouble long enough to vote?"

"Eddie," Sahara said, "tell us how this nippy weather makes you homesick for Omaha."

Eddie's response, "If mushrooms can taste good after growing in damp dark places, I can be homesick for any place I choose."

120

Crime and weather quickly gave way to seasonal thoughts.

Yancey resolved, "May the beneficiaries in my life insurance policy rejoice this morning; they're another year closer to pay day."

Since Slack wasn't present, Sahara gladly spoke for him. "May the New Year bring Slack the woman he daily longs for; one that will put him on a first-name basis with the staff at urgent care."

About 9 o'clock, the crowd scattered, leaving Eddie and Zelda to sum up the old year.

"My health has been excellent," he began, "but I'm still not fully functional with the new electric can opener."

Zelda added, "Or Netflix, or the oven."

"Your successes of course are unparalleled," he continued. "Mine are just "un.""

"As the Good Lord intended," Zelda said.

Then, without an "excuse me" or "hello," a nervous-looking fellow hurried by and asked, "Hey, got the time?"

When Eddie said nine fifteen, the fellow exhaled forcefully and moved on without a "thank you."

"You know, Zelda, it's funny," Eddie said. "Like right now, just being in a place, any place, can be helpful. And yet sometimes when Harriet and I are talking, like maybe in the kitchen, her tone seems to say that I should really be somewhere else doing something. Have you noticed that?"

Zelda welcomed the chance, "Just count the number of times that Harriet's tone has overridden anything she's saying and you've got your answer."

With his disappointment standing out like a Christmas candle in the dark, Eddie said, "Why do you do this to me, even on Christmas?"

"I do it because you're a compulsive worrier, a "freta-holic." You worry about kids who don't know who fought the War of the Roses."

That was the problem. Eddie was too good at worrying about the wrong things. But he didn't want to be real good at very much.

121

Rex, the judge, was so good at making others dislike him that when people saw him in blue sportswear, they began to dislike the color blue.

"Look," Zelda went on, "when we get home, vacuum your entire body; then cover it with Ben Gay. Maybe that will draw this worry bug out. Oh wait, I forgot–then you'll worry about where the bug went."

When The Time Comes

Chapter 30

"Time is either your friend or your enemy, regardless of who you are or where you're going." An old cowboy philosopher said that to Eddie and Harriet when they were in their early 30's and new to the high desert of southern Arizona. The old timer had worked cattle so many years that he, the saddle, and his horse looked all of one piece. "You can get bored or drunk or rich but nobody gets through without getting something," Eddie remembered him saying as he showed them what 50 years of working cattle had done to his knuckles.

The years, short though they were by comparison, had introduced Zelda to the importance of timeouts. When those breaks became more frequent, Eddie, now 72, scheduled special radiographic imaging with Dr. Ben Wilbur. Regular check-ups had not revealed any serious health problems, leaving Eddie to believe that her future would be much like her past.

Three days later, he and Zelda waited in Wilbur's office for the results; they would soon learn how an enlarged heart in a six-year-old dog would change things before either had another birthday.

"Your dog doesn't like the slick floors, does she?" asked the graying man in a pearl-button shirt and a cowboy hat waiting next to Eddie.

"It's funny," Eddie said, "we have tile at the house, but this is different."

"She's not dumb," the lean-looking gentleman said, "she stepped right on the scale all by herself."

Eddie nodded and forced a smile.

"This old Shepherd here on my foot is Hiram," he added, "he's named after Hank Williams–the old man, not the kid." When Eddie looked puzzled, the rancher said Hiram, not Hank or Henry, was the honky-tonk man's real name.

When the man learned Zelda's name, he gave his own, Francisco, and said, "Bet you a cup of coffee you're a book guy."

"Well sort of," Eddie said. "How'd you know?"

"You don't pick a name like Zelda when you rope steers for a living."

Eddie didn't say that Zelda had her name before she got to Arizona.

"Who trims your dog's toenails?" Francisco asked. "They're short."

"I do, with a grinder. It works well. The manufacturer calls it a cordless rotary tool but it's just a grinder."

"What do you think about that, Hiram?" Francisco asked. "Want one of those?"

Zelda thought, *Pretend it hurts; it'll get you big-time treats.*

"I'm pretty handy with that little gadget," Eddie said, trying to forget why he was there. "I offer the Westminster Look or the Pima County Special, whatever suits you and your dog."

Francisco said he heard of a vet over in New Mexico who did nails real well but going to see him was "a little out of the way."

Is your dog in for his shots?" Eddie asked.

"No, he's in for a sip from the Fountain of Youth—he has arthritis."

As Francisco stood up, tall and a little bent, he said, "Got a little of that myself." Pointing toward Hiram to stay put, Francisco strolled across the waiting room to the water fountain. Eddie noticed the engraving on the back of his leather belt, "Steer University." Retired humanities professors like a man who re-mixes the language a little.

As Eddie alternated between stroking Zelda's ears and flashing back in time, he thought how rewarded he felt on those early days when she didn't chew up a bush and how Harriet scolded them both when their new puppy tracked mud into the house during the monsoon. However the mud got from the yard to the house, Eddie always blamed it on the dog. "You know, Zelda," he would say, "if you had feathers and could fly, we wouldn't have this mess."

Eddie's nervousness caught the attention of a woman to his right. "Say, I don't think I've seen you here before; you appear to be worried about something. Is your house upside down, like mine?" she asked.

"Oh, I'm sorry, no it's not," Eddie said.

"I quit letting things worry me 13 years ago when my riding club elected me president," the woman said. "They blamed me for the guest speakers, the donuts, the room was too hot or too cold, and maybe even the rate of inflation. And I thought they were my friends."

Eddie was quick to express his regrets.

"And I learned a lot from that."

Zelda, thinking the woman might have overheard Eddie's conversation with Francisco, feared she would enumerate the many things that can be learned outside college classrooms.

"After four years of listening to them bitch and whine," she said, "my skin was so thick I would have made a fine county school superintendent."

Eddie made a mental note to remind Harriet how smart she was to abandon her interest in riding clubs twenty years before.

"But much more important than that...."

Eddie made a second note, to thank God if He would limit this woman's report to no more than 40 seconds.

"I learned that a dog is a much better friend than a human be-ing–any dog in this room would do. With a person, everything goes along for a few months; you're listening to your new friend's life story and all the things his mother used to say, and what happens?"

Eddie's counting on you, God, Zelda thought.

"You think you get to know somebody pretty good and then, sure as hell, one day you say to yourself, 'This guy is getting weirder and weirder.'"

Eddie bounced up the second the assistant called his name and thanked God, as promised.

In his consultation room, Dr. Wilbur said, "Eddie, we've known each other how many years now, 12 or more? And no veterinarian ever wanted to give a man bad news about his dog."

Eddie didn't mean it but he said, "Just give it to me straight, Ben."

Wilbur pointed to the images on the wall and said, "Okay, Zelda has an enlarged heart. Medically, it's called dilated cardio-myopathy. Dogs get that sometimes when they're around six or eight. Has she been a little short of breath lately?"

"I don't think so. As you know, she's never been overweight—no leftovers."

"We're not sure what causes it; maybe it's genetic."

Wilbur explained that the condition can lead to congestive heart failure and that drugs were available that might enhance her heart contractions but there was no known cure.

"Okay," Eddie said quickly, "then she can still live a normal life, right?"

"That's right Eddie, but I have to be honest. In general, life expectancy in these cases is from six months to two years, depending upon a dog's overall health, which in Zelda's case is excellent."

Eddie couldn't look at anything but the images. "So you're saying there's nothing we can do."

"I'm sorry," Wilbur said, "after twenty years, I never seem to get this quite right. There are a couple of things. Keep Zelda on low-sodium dog food, and don't let her over- exercise or become suddenly excited."

Eddie was bluffing, "No more growling at Javelinas, Kid."

"If you want another opinion, I'll send a full report anywhere you want."

With his interest in dog-owner psychology, Wilbur knew some of them always hope for miracles, others try to hide their feelings and no preparation for such losses carries a guarantee. He wasn't a therapist or a counselor but he knew that the comfort of the victims has to come as much from them as from others. Still wishing it could have been otherwise, Wilbur put his hand on Eddie's shoulder and said, "Whenever it happens, Eddie, there won't be any charges for my part."

Zelda was quiet, almost like she hadn't heard anything.

As Eddie and Zelda walked back to the lobby, the assistant was handing Francisco the medication that would knock out most of Hiram's pain. She said it wouldn't make the old boy any younger but it would make him feel younger and that was the important thing.

"I've been around animal owners too long not to see what you're thinking," Francisco said. "You're going to lose her, right?"

Eddie summed up Wilbur's diagnosis as he led Zelda to the car.

"We're strangers, but I'd like to say a couple of things, if it's alright?" Francisco asked.

"Anything at all will be helpful."

"When the time comes, you do whatever you need to do," Francisco said. "Don't be afraid to show how much you liked that dog. It's nobody else's business. Play some of your favorite songs from high school, plant some roses. But don't ever catch a bad case of self-pity. Your friends will get tired of it, and it won't bring your dog back."

Eddie marveled at how much a man could say in half a minute.

Francisco shifted the way he was leaning against the pickup before making his last point.

"When I first began ranching, I thought you handled life's problems the way you branded cattle–one at a time and on to the next one. Then when my wife died eight years ago, I could see

127

that the branding comparison I had going wasn't worth a damn. Good friends tried to make me feel better, telling me this would pass. They meant well, but when a man's wife dies you shouldn't tell him he'll get over it."

Eddie hadn't missed a single syllable.

"And whatever problems like that are to you, that's how big they are, no matter what anybody says. So, whatever this dog is to you, that's where you start."

Eddie, surrounded by books all of his life, had not found what this man had found on a ranch thirty miles from anywhere. He thought, *if I ever try to say how I feel about this, I'll make it short.*

"Oh, and if you're up there on that narrow road leading to Wells Corners," Francisco said as he turned the ignition in his pickup, "look for a small sign that says, 'Lopez.' Stop in."

I Understand These Things

Chapter 31

On the Saturday following the bad news from the veterinarian, Eddie and Zelda went to a small park so they could see Mount Whitlow with its tall pines and wonder how the defective heart of a dog fits into the mystery of life.

The Work Projects Administration (WPA) built the park in the 1930s and named it Hyde Park, after President Franklin Delano Roosevelt's home on the Hudson River. One of the few pieces left of its physical history, a broken entrance sign, had been altered to read, "Damn Your Hide Park." Eddie guessed the controversy over The New Deal might still be alive.

Before Eddie actually began to look for meaning in death and dying, Zelda said, "Look Cowboy, save yourself a lot of work, and save me a lot of embarrassment. Make very short speeches, and make them to the living, not the dying. Maybe just talk to yourself—or to ducks. And if you want to say something important, say how my fame rescued you from obscurity."

"I'm just trying to do what's appropriate at a time like this," Eddie said.

"Then don't start trying to define me. People are always telling me who I am. I arrived in Tucson partly because JD said you worried more than a Popsicle at a July cook-out and you needed

129

a distraction."

"Well, I think we should have a memorial maybe with candles and old pictures."

"My goodness, and then somebody will say how much they'll miss me and how they'd like it if dogs could live forever."

"What's so bad about that?"

"Just this, when I was a year old you went on about your rights as owner of the bushes and trees in the backyard."

"They were mine."

"Right, but this time I'm the owner–of myself. My life and death are mine, so no long ceremony, you hear me?"

"It all seems so empty without a tribute."

"Okay," Zelda said, "then take a minute to apologize for all the times you treated me like a dog."

"Real funny, Zelda," Eddie said, "but if you were being treated like a dog, that was the time to start talking to somebody else."

Still unwilling to give the matter the grim sobriety that it usually gets, Zelda said, "We could settle all this very easily, you know; just saddle up and we'll ride off together."

"I can't go now," Eddie said. "Harriet and I have to take care of each other for a while."

"Yeah, and two years from now, when somebody tells you Rex the judge came back to life, you'll say, "Damn, I should have gone with Zelda when I had the chance."

"Good point."

"Okay," Zelda said, "then here's my final offer. You and Harriet take my ashes to Big Icicle and spread them on Ghost Dance Lake. They'll be safe from traffic and other racket and you can stop by if you're in the area."

Eddie's thoughts flew ahead to the times when he would go up to strangers walking their dogs and begin, *I had a dog once; her name was Zelda.*

"And on those early mornings when you're sitting on the glider," Zelda said, "and a small white cloud drifts across the Catalina Mountains, you can look up, wave your hand and say,

'Good morning, Ms. "C." You're looking really fluffy today. When you pass over The Black Hills of South Dakota, would you stop and say hello to Zelda?' "

As the news about Zelda became harder to manage, Eddie was relieved to see two people from his block, Bunny and her four-year-old daughter, Emma, at the picnic table near the end of the park.

When Henry, Emma's blue parakeet died, her father, Wilson, told her how important good friends like Henry are, but that sometimes when they get sick they "don't make it." He assured her that Henry was in a new place and that when she got older, she would "understand these things." Emma listened intently and responded with her usual, "For sure, Dad."

At times like that, Wilson's balance between candor and caution could have become the standard for young parents everywhere. At others, his passion for an issue or a duty overwhelmed the matters themselves. Bunny, on the other hand, voted on the caution side every time and wished her daughter would not repeat everything exactly as her dad said it. Eddie wished that he would live long enough to find out how this young family would turn out.

After a couple of "hi's" and "how are you's," Emma opened her four-year-old repertoire of Wilson-like candor with, "My dad says Zelda's got a bum heart."

Surprised, Eddie said, "That's correct, her heart isn't working quite right."

Confident that she knew most of what was coming, Zelda dozed intermittently under a nearby table.

"Can she get fixed up?" Emma asked.

"Dr. Wilbur is talking that over with other veterinarians," Eddie tried.

"I hope she doesn't have to go to Boston to get fixed up," Emma said.

"Why is that?" Eddie asked.

"My dad says the place is full of Irishmen."

"Emma, Sweetheart," Bunny said hurriedly. "Your dad was

131

just kidding. Irishmen work very hard and they sing the most beautiful songs in the world."

"If Zelda doesn't make it, Mr. Grace," Emma said, "will you make a speech like my dad did when Henry died?"

"I don't know if I can do that as well as your dad did; he's an awful good talker."

"After my dad's speech, we clapped for Henry," Emma said.

Eddie promised, "I'll do my best—and we'll clap for Zelda."

"Be sure to tell me if anything happens to Zelda, Mr. Grace, because I understand these things," Emma said,

"I'll do that, Emma. Your mother and I will work it out."

"My dad teaches me new words every day," Emma said proudly.

"He's a good dad, Emma. What word did he teach you yesterday?"

"He taught me the meaning of 'republican.'"

"That's a good word to know," Eddie said.

"For sure, Mr. Grace."

"And what did he teach you today?"

"He told me about social security."

"What did he say social security meant?" Eddie asked.

"He said it meant nobody works anymore."

"Oh for God's sake," Bunny said, "Honey, your dad exaggerates too much. You and I can talk a little more about social security tomorrow."

Almost like a fate-inspired rescue, a young boy, alone on the park swings, caught Bunny's eye and she instinctively asked Emma if she'd like to go play with him.

"Okay, Mom," Emma said. "Mr. Grace, can Zelda go along?"

With Eddie's okay, Emma roused Zelda and they ran off to the swings.

"She remembers everything her dad says," Bunny said.

"She's her daddy's daughter, that's for sure." Eddie said.

"Just last week, she toppled over with her bike. It must have been the third spill of the day or something because she jumped up and, as though she was speaking her native tongue, she said, 'damn it to hell!' I have to say I laughed to myself."

"As much as I'd like to," Eddie said, "I won't bring up the bike today."

"What will you do for Zelda after she's gone?" Bunny asked.

"Harriet and I have been asking that same question."

"Do let us know what you decide. Ever since we lost Henry, Emma has been talking a lot about Zelda."

Then, faster than they ran toward the swings, Emma and Zelda ran back.

"I'm not swinging with him again," Emma said.

"What happened, Sweetheart?" Bunny asked.

"That boy is stupid, Mom. He can't do anything right. He pushes the wrong way and he gets in the road all the time. I almost decked him, didn't I, Zelda?"

Zelda wagged her tail in agreement.

Eddie regretted that Wilson wasn't there to hear how Emma hung on his every word.

The Commissioner Of Dreams

Chapter 32

Knowing that Zelda would never be well again, Eddie searched for something that could transcend the hard scientific facts of electronic imaging and Dr. Wilbur's diagnosis. If he couldn't dent the truth in the pictures, at least he wanted someone to tell him whose purposes were served by the early death of a beautiful and loving dog. If he could find some good in that, he would shout it to the world, not just once but a thousand times.

It wasn't that he and Harriet had not been around death before. When you're past 70, you've gone to a lot of funerals, heard a lot of eulogies and expressed your regrets to a lot of survivors. They respected whatever services each family chose for such occasions. Music at funerals moved Eddie especially, whether it was "Bridge Over Troubled Water" or "The Battle Hymn of the Republic" or "Ave Maria."

Neither he nor Harriet ever hid the personal fulfillment they felt each year when they visited the small country cemeteries where many of their family members were buried. Since grade school, they had accepted the union of mystery and actuality in discussions of death. More than once they had talked of building a suitable memorial in their backyard for Zelda.

Over the years, the Graces became more confident that the

bond between the living and the dead shifted at death but did not break. And a physical presence–a gravesite with a marker–was crucial to lives lived simultaneously in the past, present and future. With those beliefs almost second nature, any doubts about a place for Zelda that they could see and touch never arose until the day Zelda told Eddie that she wanted her ashes left at Ghost Dance Lake.

One evening, Eddie sat alone on the glider, replaying Dr. Wilbur's discovery of Zelda's heart condition as he watched the reds and blues come and go in the Catalina Mountains. Harriet was returning phone calls and Zelda, according to her custom, had retired early. Before long, he began thinking, *How do we handle a dog's need to be buried 1,400 miles away? How do I explain that the whereabouts of Zelda's ashes is not a decision for Harriet and me alone?*

The answer came easily, but as always, before Eddie really had an answer, he had more questions. This usually meant delays, possible reversals and quite often a rescue by Harriet. Eddie never fully grasped the idea that labor, even intellectual labor, should bear fruit, not just more labor.

This time, Eddie began well ahead of his usual starting points of history and precedents: *At some time in his life*, he thought, *a man becomes the commissioner of dreams, a speculator in folktales, a myth practitioner. He doesn't always need a big myth, like Manifest Destiny; just a little one, maybe something like those about cottontail rabbits. I wouldn't want a myth that makes people dangerous or crazy. I couldn't believe one that turns believers into fanatics.*

Eddie wasn't thinking of a myth that triggered a global review of animal rights–just a little scrap of ideology to cover one dog's wishes. A man who thinks the familiar sound of phone books dropping at his door is soothing is neither a founding father nor a rebel.

And Eddie sure didn't want a myth based upon some kind of clear deception, but he could live with one that had a part or two missing–incomplete, sort of. At his age, he was ready to find consolation in folklore, where the storyteller isn't bound by the usual constraints of logic, consistency and rules of evidence. Folklorists have no borders to defend, no committees to consult. Their art needs no official certification; it only needs to work.

Yancey, he thought, *knew that the importance of a folktale lies not in the truth; it lies in the telling. In the land of stories, there's no place for arguments that only wear out the very thing being talking about. In myths, it's not important that your head be on straight. It's only important that your head be comfortable, however it's on.*

Nobody Trips On A Rainbow

Chapter 33

"You've been out here a long time, Dear," Harriet said, "would you like a glass of wine?"

"That sounds great. I've been trying to remember, wasn't it one of those "headband" poets of the Sixties who said since this world makes no promises of its own, our imaginations fly us away to places that do?"

Harriet sensed that, with a little push from her, the matter of Zelda's memorial might soon be resolved and that the resolution would include singularity and some notion of duty. She remembered Eddie's admiration for Socrates who, just after he had drunk the hemlock, reminded his aide, "Crito, we owe a cock to Asclepius; do pay the debt."

"Something appropriate for the Queen of Hearts Landing," Harriet said as she set out two small glasses of a wine she had bought that afternoon, "after all, Zelda never actually knocked the mayor down. He just fell into the vertical blinds when she tried to give him a kiss."

Eddie was pleased that she had, not unexpectedly, found a balance between the recent bad news and the joy that Zelda had given them. Harriet, hoping to build on her suggestion, said she had thought of a special service for Zelda, "but if you remember, the blessing she received as a puppy was pretty slow-acting. For two years, I thought the power of Father Ragone's right arm had missed its mark entirely."

True to his professional instincts and despite his new-found interest in the power of folk recipes, Eddie briefly veered again toward the language of rights–natural, lost, forgotten and future.

Pulling him back to something more immediate, Harriet asked, "Why do loving and attentive wives of 40-plus years pour red wine into empty glasses, and their husbands get called bread winners and heads of the house? When do the better halves get to talk?"

Embarrassed but apt, Eddie said he meant to include a wife's right to speak her piece under "momentarily-overlooked" rights.

Harriet, as always, moved with a purpose.

"We lay our loved ones to rest in expensive places and then spend a billion dollars every Memorial Day on flowers to tell them we haven't forgotten them. We build shrines, establish foundations and write books, all to show off the importance of our forbears."

"Perfect," Eddie said. "The deceased have rights, but we always limit those rights to people, our kind, and forget that the rights of dogs are also important."

"Customs outlive their origins," Harriet said, "and fast or slow, they change, get eulogized and left behind–buried, if you will."

"And we renew the debate over replacements for those customs," Eddie added.

"Some men chase dreams, like a hole in one or an Emmy nomination," Harriet said. "Others feel lucky if they get socks that fit. There's no need to analyze it or seek public approval for how we handle this memorial."

"That makes sense."

"Eddie, good sense is not the issue. One man builds a shrine for a saint. That's his dream. A few years later, another dreamer comes along, buys the property and starts a horse farm. That's how life goes."

"You're right," Eddie said. "We should leave Zelda's ashes at Ghost Dance Lake, because it was her favorite place, and her right to be left there shouldn't end when her heart stops."

"Zelda," Harriet said, "gave us a new life for six years; now it's time to let her go."

Then without another word, Harriet dashed into the house and brought out a small green cardboard box that she had kept in her dresser for three years.

"I think we grew up some tonight," she said as she opened the box and showed Eddie the sliver of buffalo skin that Little Oak had sent back with them from Big Icicle. "How much you can learn after being on social security for years. It's almost funny, but look at this."

"Let buffalo roam," Eddie read the words under his breath.

"Three years ago in the canoe, Little Oak put those words into my hand and said a message would come to us–not to go hunting for it–and we would know the moment it arrived. She said it would come in simple words, like 'til we meet again' or 'I love you.'"

"I remember." Eddie said. "She also said 'don't try to guess it. This is not *What's My Line.*'"

Eddie Grace didn't ordinarily hunt for hidden messages concealed in sudden storms or sleepless nights. He had plenty of trouble with events that were clear and seen by others. But with Little Oak's confidence in the power of "3" still in his memory, he watched Harriet pour the last of the wine into his glass and said, "If you tell me that's three ounces, I'm in."

"Eddie," Harriet said. "'Let her go' is the message. I just said it, or it found me, or us, a minute ago. Three little words; that's it." As she spoke, she wrote "let her go" on the back of the buffalo skin.

And so from Zelda's heart condition and their anxiety over a place for her ashes, a new world of myth and mystery called to the Graces. Stories that filled the vacuum between science and the distress over a lost loved one. Eddie had listened to Yancey long enough to believe that the American Dream was a fable and the free market system little more than a declaration of economic war, but in their time and place, they worked. "*The entire world, both before and after Zelda,"* Eddie thought, *"is made up of no more than a grain of truth for every bushel of fiction, but if that works what's the problem?"*

Zelda and Little Oak were real, true, like science, but Eddie suddenly found it easy to embellish the last six years with fiction of his own: *Once in a land very far away,* he thought, *there lived a beautiful young dog with a bright gold coat. Her name was Zelda, and she could talk. She took long walks with her friend, Edward. They talked about trees and bushes and chickens and airplanes, and married people and baseball. When Zelda's life ended, Edward and Harriet carried her ashes back to the place she loved most and laid them on the cool, still water of Ghost Dance Lake because she had earned that right.*

"And another thing," Harriet said as she picked up the wine glasses. "Don't go to the Wren tomorrow looking for more advice on what to do. If you want excellent advice, just relax those rules for correct thinking. Two adults and a dog are quite enough to get this right. How many opinions did you get when we got married? God, I don't want to know."

For half a century, Eddie had thought myths were inspiring but somehow always in another time and place; never here today where you could unwrap them. He believed folklore was unsafe for regular use and that the factual information we had was sufficient to answer everyday questions. More than once, he had said our dearest folktales were like rainbows; they were beautiful but always just out of reach.

But then along came a very hard decision about life and death. A decision that took him away from what's practical and customary and into the fantastic land of riddles, secrets and yes, rainbows. And he welcomed the thought that nobody trips on a rainbow.

Eddie overheard Harriet as she passed Zelda's pillow, "Go to sleep, Honey. Your buddy will be ready for your walk in the morning."

Get A Deaf Bird

Chapter 34

With hope and an emerging myth, the Graces watched and waited for anything that might signal a change in Zelda's condition. They searched the internet, read the *Arizona Daily Star* front to back, and asked every person they knew about heart failure in dogs. One morning, Eddie got up at the usual time for Zelda's walk, 5 a.m., turned on a TV news channel and saw four deputy sheriffs with guns drawn making an arrest in Phoenix. He thought how he would welcome a headline like, "Heart failure taken into custody late yesterday." But that wasn't to be, and Eddie continued to scrutinize Zelda constantly for evidence of fatigue or disorientation.

The summer monsoon is well known for its sharp claps of thunder, especially in Arizona's higher elevations, and Harriet wisely kept Zelda indoors and raised the volume on soft music to make the seasonal storms seem farther away.

On July 12, 2011, such a splash of monsoon splendor dropped two inches of rain on Hearts Landing in less than an hour. The downpour filled the arroyos to capacity, signaled the frogs to croak their annual arias, and left minor wind damage in several areas of town. When the skies cleared, Eddie and Zelda took an extra walk, inhaling the clean air and sidestepping storm debris.

"So will you get another dog when I'm gone?" Zelda asked.

"I really haven't thought about that, but let me answer your question the way I did when Harriet asked me if I would ever marry again. I said, 'Sweetheart, having had one wife, who would want another?'"

"You're smart," Zelda said, "another dog would never work. Any animal worth a dime would run off the moment you started on one of your pure theories. Next time you need a companion, get a deaf bird."

"Excuse me, but you think I'm also a throwback, don't you?" Eddie asked.

"Well, you're a philosopher, I figure you're a throwback to some place that nobody ever heard of or cares to. Is it true that you made a living just wondering about things like purpose and meaning?"

"To tell the truth, in six years I spent much of my time wondering which bush in the backyard would be the next one to go."

"Lately," Zelda said, "I've been wondering where I came from—not Big Icicle, I mean where did the first one of me come from. But I'm not going to ask anybody because in Hearts Landing alone I've heard a dozen different stories on how people got started."

"So, did you ever hear a story you liked?" Eddie asked.

"I did as a matter of fact. It was a short thing, told by a cheese salesman at Gus's place. He was almost as crazy as JD. You were in the bathroom."

"Sorry I missed it," Eddie said. "Tell me."

"Okay, the cheese salesman said long before clocks and calendars, God had this huge chunk of cheese in His pantry that He always thought He would do something with. It looked a lot like those triangular things that Wisconsinites wear on their heads at football games, only much bigger. And God thought this would be a good place for people to live, so he took his index finger and poked a lot of holes in the cheese for houses and gave everybody free rent for the first three months.

"The salesman said everything was going along fine until one day a couple of philosophers said how there had to be something more to life than holes in cheese. And then a week later, a woman obsessed with social ranking, complained that the place God had given her was on a bad street."

"I don't believe your cheese story for one minute," Eddie said, "but you've got a great yarn going. What happened next?"

"The salesman said God got angry as hell and melted all the cheese. So the people had to find new places to live. Some went to North Dakota where they learned that steady work could warm their houses and fill their souls with a spirit of self-reliance. Some of the rest went to Texas where the men especially took to wearing large white hats and saying 'Darlin' a lot."

"Ya know, I think Harriet and I heard that word "Darlin'" more than once the last time we drove through Amarillo," Eddie said.

"Then the salesman said these people who had been deported because they screwed up the free rent, saw all of this as part of a clear plan especially for them and they began telling their kids and grandkids the great story of cheese."

"But didn't anybody at Gus's ask where the cheese came from," Eddie asked, "and what it all meant?"

"Just one guy from Missouri; he called it baloney. But the salesman was ready. He said, 'Hey, lighten up. We don't know what it all means. If it meant anything, it would be worth something, and if it was worth something, I'd be selling it.' And then he snapped his brief case shut and walked out."

When a dude in a purple-and-orange 70s pickup honked and splashed a small puddle of rain water on them, Zelda said, "What do you think, Cowboy, was that a hard working dude from Dakota or a darlin' guy from Amarillo? Wherever he's from, I'll bet he hasn't asked about the meaning of cheese since the day he started shaving."

Zelda asked Eddie if he could remember the last time he honked at somebody just for the hell of it. When he said he couldn't, Zelda reminded him, "It was five years ago when you took your 87-year-old mother-in-law for a ride in a '67 Karmann Ghia convertible and the old lady sang, "Way Down Upon The Swampy River." My apologies to Dixie."

To her list of fun people, Zelda added the cookie lady who carried treats in her fanny pack for dogs along the morning walks. She never asked for the dogs' affection or wondered if giving free cookies meant something "more." And Zelda said Lilac, the poor thing, might be just another person who took a couple of wrong turns in the cheese run.

"The important thing that you keep forgetting," Zelda said, "is that, while philosophers stay stuck in the past, the people keep redefining the big things. Every week we get something new to honk about."

"For instance?" Eddie challenged.

"Just in the last century, they broadened the definition of patriotism, opened the pearly gates a little wider and gave us some believable explanations for mental and emotional disorders. And then there's the really big one—the one that said women could be just as free as the guys. Free to use their birth names, run for public office, become doctors and to ride motorcycles."

"So what are you and I redefining right now?"

"Simple, you're trying–off and on, at least–to support people who are in low-paying jobs, and I'm asking for a new entitlement program for dogs–dead dogs."

Then in less than two minutes, the loving, sometimes contentious relationship between a dog lost in time and a normally-impaired philosopher came to an abrupt end. A city maintenance truck on clean-up duty after the rain veered to miss a pothole and hurled a trash-can lid to within four feet of Zelda. Her heart stopped as suddenly as Dr. Wilbur said it might. Instinctively, she squeezed tightly against Eddie, the way she did during her first three nights in Arizona. Trembling, Eddie promised, "We will take you home to Ghost Dance Lake." Zelda closed her eyes and she was gone.

Explanations for untimely losses of life are usually attempted by poets and ministers, but this time Eddie didn't reach for anybody else's answers to why he and Zelda and the truck were in the same place that stormy day. Instead, he pictured life as a mysterious coming and going of highs and lows.

The truck driver stopped immediately, rushed up to Eddie and asked if Zelda was alright. Eddie shook his head.

"I'm so sorry," the driver said, "please let me give you my card. The city has insurance that will cover the loss of your dog. We've seen you walking together a hundred times."

Eddie said, "Thank you very much Sir, but money wouldn't really make any difference."

Will Zelda See Henry?

Chapter 35

Eddie had gradually come to believe that myths and folklore are handy, even necessary, because of our preference for stories that meet our needs. He believed that fictional accounts, like make-up, perform a work that truth never can.

Four-year-old Emma was lucky enough to be surrounded by loved ones who chose their myths carefully and waited for the right time to acknowledge the world's harsher side. She hadn't yet heard about foreclosures or the frightening details of Alzheimer's, so when it became necessary to tell her the story of Zelda's death, her mother asked Eddie to stop by. He chose Thursday morning just before Emma's "Kudos for Kiddos" class because then there wouldn't be much time for the hard questions that four-year olds ask.

"I'm so glad you came over, Eddie," Bunny said. "Emma will be here in a minute."

"No hurry," Eddie said.

"She received kudos this year for never being late to a class. Her dad always emphasizes being on time."

"That's a good idea," Eddie said.

"I should add that he also stressed punctuality for the teacher."

"That's Wilson."

When Emma came into the living room with a cheery "Good morning, Mr. Grace," Eddie asked her what she was going to do in class that day. She said, "We're going to hear Mr. Sebastian."

"Bach," Bunny clarified.

"My dad doesn't care much for him; says he makes people nervous."

Eddie knew delaying wouldn't make this any easier.

"Emma," he asked, "do you remember in the park when we talked about Henry, and your dad said he went home?"

Emma looked straight ahead and said, "for sure, Mr. Grace."

"Well three days ago, Zelda's heart couldn't work any longer and she went home," Eddie said as bravely as he could.

"Oh," Emma said with a mixture of wonder and uncertainty.

"Emma, Honey," Bunny said, "it's okay. Zelda is safe."

Emma thought a moment and then asked, "Will Zelda see Henry?"

"Zelda and Henry are both home," Eddie said.

"Mr. Grace, can we clap now for Zelda, the way we clapped for Henry?" Emma asked.

"Let's all clap for Zelda now," Bunny said.

The living room clock said Kudos class started in 10 minutes.

Emma kissed her mother and said, "I have to go or I'll be late. Goodbye, Mr. Grace. I love you, Zelda."

Individual Results May Vary

Chapter 36

Before the flight left that would take Zelda's ashes back to Ghost Dance Lake, Eddie became more apprehensive than usual. He and Harriet had never accompanied a loved one's remains before and each step in the process added to the strain on their emotions. He stewed over lost luggage, pilot error, violent thunderstorms in the Heartland, everything.

He also worried about what he would say at the lakeside service. At his father's funeral, he described him as poor and ever mindful of his duties as a husband and parent. He said his dad had never written two checks for more than a thousand dollars.

But he couldn't say things like that about a dog, and he sure couldn't say how Zelda always had a good word for everyone. He couldn't do much with her career or community service in the usual sense. Eddie's upbringing hadn't prepared him to talk about an animal's soul heading home the way Fr. Ragone talked about the soul of Eileen O'Donnell. He needed simple words and not too many of them.

After Eddie had talked to himself about the services for Zelda, he stopped at the Wren to ask the "heads of state" for suggestions regarding Zelda's eulogy. He second-guessed that decision when

Slack advised, "Just think of a few old girlfriends and something will come right to you."

Sahara asked, "Would somebody please tell this man to get professional help?"

A new customer suggested a holy card with a bird sitting on Saint Francis' shoulder. Eddie thanked the woman, but to be more personal he said he'd look for the picture he took of Zelda and Emma a year before. Gus said the next chair donated would honor the Queen of Hearts Landing. The six-year habit of having Zelda with him at the café made Eddie reach for her leash as he stood up to leave. The regulars saw his embarrassment and wisely said nothing.

At home, Eddie called JD to confirm the travel plans.

"I don't know if I told you," JD said, "at Sioux Falls, I'll be picking you up at a private landing strip, not far from the main terminal."

"Are they doing repairs or what?" Eddie asked.

"No repairs, Buddy. It's faster and the shuttle goes right by there. It's a kind of "drop in/slide in" place that I use whenever I can."

"Whatever you say," Eddie said.

"And if one of us is early, there's a cute little café real close to the runway. If they had a drive-up window, I think I could pop in there without coming to a complete stop. I spent four years testing fighter planes for Uncle Sam, you know."

JD then said he had something that he had to see his publisher about and Eddie regretted that they had not inquired about a bus from Sioux Falls to Rapid City.

When Harriet asked if the flight was still on, Eddie told her JD said everything was under control. She had made all the other arrangements for the trip, including a sky-blue carrying case for Zelda's ashes and a wallet-size picture of her at Ghost Dance Lake taped to the side.

On route to South Dakota, Eddie and Harriet distracted themselves talking about federal relief programs in the 30s, "shoebox

149

radios" and the mysterious strength that kept their parents from feeling cheated by the Great Depression.

The flight took them over sections of Kansas Highway 54 where they strained to pick out what looked like wheat fields. Eddie, with fifty years of books and classrooms in his resume, said, "that's what they call applied philosophy–everything makes sense down there except the weather and the government's red tape." They remembered how Catholic wives often worried that their husbands were better acquainted with bourbon whiskey than holy water.

Over eastern Nebraska, the pilot dropped altitude slightly to give the passengers a better feel for rural life. He had to be from a farm out there somewhere. Closer to the ground, Eddie fancied that he saw his old baseball diamond. He thought, *those weeds-and-dirt playing fields were "Yankee Stadium" to anybody well enough off to own a glove.* Forever a make-mine-Midwest kind of man, he said to the stranger in the seat across from him, "And when a little guy in one of those towns talks to his teammates about their next ballgame and says, 'my dad will be there,' his dad will be there."

As they passed Sioux City, Iowa and neared the Sioux Falls terminal, the pilot announced, "The air must be lighter today Without help from a tailwind, we used nearly five percent less fuel than on any trip I can recall."

Arriving ahead of schedule, Harriet and Eddie had time to kill while they waited for JD. They grabbed the shuttle that JD mentioned and were dropped off at the small café. When Harriet eyed the name, the Bali Lo, and asked the driver "are you sure this is the place?" the driver answered, "Oh, this is the place, alright; there aren't any other places out here."

The building's sagging roof lines and a gravel parking lot suggested either a throwback to the 30s or bankruptcy. Much against her will, Harriet went in but only after Eddie promised that this was coffee and absolutely nothing on a plate.

Once again, Harriet was right. The first sound inside the place was "Welcome to Sioux Falls' finest one-star clubhouse! What'll it be, Folks?"

Harriet blurted out, "Nothing for me, I'm fasting."

Eddie ordered coffee and skipped the cream and sugar. The Wren seemed suddenly okay.

Harriet asked. "Did you happen to notice that small "item" on the ground just outside the door?" When Eddie said he did, Harriet said, "That wasn't French pastry! Or maybe that's the 'cute' part that JD referred to."

"You from around here?" asked a customer at one of the four tables.

Despite Eddie's preference for cafes with "home cooking" across the top of the menu, the situation didn't seem right for socializing. "Uh, no we're not," he answered.

"Where you from?"

"We're from Ari…"

"Where in Arizona?"

Harriet said, "Hearts Landing."

"Never heard of it. I got an in-law down there somewhere who says he doesn't know where Sioux Falls, South Dakota is. Can you believe that? He doesn't get around much."

"Well, that can happen," Eddie said. "Staying put is kind of like being married to the right woman. If you like where you are, you don't go looking for something else." He was hoping to recover some of Harriet's good will.

"Hey, that's damned good. I'm Elbert, with an 'E.' What do you do down there in, what did you say, Heartsville?"

"Hearts Landing," Eddie answered. "I'm a retired teacher."

"Teacher of what?"

"Philosophy, at a community college."

"Oh shit, did you hear that, Norbert," Elbert yelled to one of his two friends. Norbert shook his head, "no."

"I went to college once," Elbert said, "a new place they built when I was living up in Willow Flats."

Eddie asked how he liked school.

151

"Not one damned bit. I quit after three days and got my money back. Didn't have nothin' there I was interested in."

Harriet said, "That was before the college put in the pool tables."

"So what brings you this far up north?"

Eddie couldn't tell who asked the question; the customers' lips didn't move much.

"We're meeting a friend of mine," Eddie answered, "JD from a small town near Rapid City."

Elbert looked at his buddies and laughed, "Oh, we all know him. Don't believe a word he says."

Harriet answered, "We'll keep that in mind."

"And keep this too," Elbert said as he handed Eddie a business card. "That's my personal card. Next time you get up this way, I'll take you out to lunch in a nice place. Every time I come to this place, they throw pickles all over my cheeseburger; I hate those damned pickles."

Eddie restrained a chuckle and said, "I'll get the waitress; maybe they have some regular pickles."

When the wind blew the screen door open, Harriet said, "Edward," (official for 'Eddie') "if you *ever* drag me into another place like this, I'm filing."

Eddie knew he needed to get out of the Bali Lo while he was still married.

Just then a scraping noise, some dust and what sounded like a blown tire came from the landing strip. Eddie's new friend guessed, "That's either JD or the start of the General Resurrection." Eddie bounced up as if he'd just won the lottery.

The plane had no identification or logos that he could make out through the Bali Lo windows; just one large, orange message on the fuselage reading, "The Duct Tape Special." Looking to distance himself while Harriet dropped three dollars on the table, Eddie stepped outside quickly and looked hard at the plane.

When JD got out, Eddie asked, "What kind of plane is this? Who made it?"

"Made?" JD repeated. "You mean like manufacturer? I'm not sure who the first maker was. I re-made it here and there a few times. Didn't I tell you the plane was custom?"

"Where did you get the money to do that?" Eddie asked.

"Investors, mainly."

"Like who?"

"Like about-to-be-discovered entrepreneurs."

"You got a name or a company?" Again for the sake of the marriage.

Knowing how many questions Eddie might have about air safety, Harriet found a bench under a nearby tree.

"No big names," JD said, "but let me tell you about my ex-mother-in-law, a wheeler/dealer who used to stay in an assisted living place over in Pierre. She had this gold bridge on the lower left that was a little loose and she said she didn't need it for the chicken noodle soup the place served. So she asked me if I wanted to put it to some good use."

"You took the woman's bridge?"

"She said the thing wasn't doing her any good. It was just a lid sitting on top of an old root. A chunk of gold that size gets you bucks down in Rapid. Her bridge and a couple of lucky antique dealers are the reasons I don't need to charge my friends for a ride."

"What exactly did you buy?" Eddie asked.

This was just what JD wanted—a chance to play the worry game with his old friend.

"I bought a lot of parts yard sales, estate sales, free on the sidewalk–strapped them all together and it flew. Sometimes I refer to this baby as my Transcontinental Arrow In Duct Tape. Sounds like a symphony, doesn't it? I'll bet you heard me when I dropped in just now, didn't you?"

After all the years, this guy is still full of surprises, Eddie thought.

"Let me fast forward. I got my own virtual reality thing that I'm working on—emphasis virtual. You want to invest?"

153

Eddie shook his head and thought, *I don't know if I want to ride in this thing.*

"Here's the deal," JD said. "People ride roller coasters to get scared, right? If they don't get scared, they want their money back."

Eddie, who rarely interrupted anybody, said, "I don't pay to get scared."

"Of course you don't," JD said. "You don't have to. I'll bet the first time you rode a tricycle you thought you were going to die on the thing, right?"

Eddie said, "I remember it well."

"But let me finish this virtual reality thing I'm thinking about. People are always looking for something that sounds a little dangerous; something they can brag about later. Well, the old Black Hills are perfect for that—unpredictable weather, natural turbulence, unexpected updrafts, lots of gorgeous scenery and historic places that people always want to get real close to.

"I'll fly them out to places that they can't drive or hike to and I'll give them a close-up that they would never get any other way. I used to spray farmers' fields, you know. If they want to tell their friends that they stared death in the face, that's their business. I'm not using the word "dangerous" one time or warning them that they might be taking their last trip "up." However, if they want to say they saw the place where Sitting Bull had a vision, that's fine."

Again Eddie interrupted, mostly to get into the plane and going. "Why don't you just put a passenger or two out on the wing, for "reality" as you call it?" Eddie asked somewhat mockingly.

Not to be outdone by Eddie's attempt at humor, JD answered, "Actually, I've decided against that; you lose somebody out there and you've shot the hell out of any repeat business from him."

Harriet could be seen looking at her watch.

Before Eddie could say all this sounded like "deception," JD said "perception" was everything and that way everybody gets what he wants.

Eddie did say, "I suppose you'll be booking in about a year, right?"

"We can do it right now. Tickets are half-price until the first lift off."

JD added that all this was still in the concept stage; Eddie checked again for anything hanging or dragging.

As Harriet made her way into the "duct tape special," she noticed a small card on the ceiling above the cockpit that read, "Nobody ever died on this plane; individual results may vary."

In five minutes, they were airborne and headed toward Potato Creek, Red Shirt and eventually Rapid City.

It wasn't long before JD tested Harriet's knowledge of the law by admitting to his habit of napping once he had reached the desired altitude. She immediately referred him to the laws against sleeping pilots and he, as planned, said he'd never "seen a law man up here."

Recognizing JD's "set up" and resigned to the impossibility of changing planes, Harriet actually settled in for a light nap before they reached the Badlands.

JD turned his attention back half a century.

"Say Ed, you still got your old charcoal suit?"

"Yes. How about you?"

"In the closet, single-breast, three buttons, notches in the lapels."

"I kept a pair of silver cuff links until Harriet gave them away at a yard sale 10 years ago," Eddie said.

"Damn, you should have brought that suit along; you could have worn it to the memorial tomorrow. You haven't gained a pound."

"Nah, I might spill something on it."

"What happened to the 50s, Ed? Was it something we did?"

"I don't think anybody knows that, JD. As much as I don't like change, you have to face it."

"Yeah, but we were happy. Everybody had a dream and one job that paid the bills, and nobody ever locked their doors."

"And you knew who you were dancing with," Eddie added with a grin.

"I wouldn't be surprised if one of these days New York sets up recovering muggers' stations. Then watch those dudes grab a free meal and somebody's wallet all in one trip."

Eddie said, "According to Harriet, the crime rate has actually dropped off significantly in the Big Apple over the last five years."

"Dropped off hell! The muggers are just checking in with their accountants. That stuff won't stop until they run out of people. Same thing out here. The coyotes hunt rabbits until they run out of them and then they look for a new spot."

"You were in New York a while, right?" Eddie asked.

"For four years after the service. Let me tell you, I feel a lot safer in this plane than I ever did on Seventh Avenue. Up here, it's just me and this old relic–well, four old relics on this trip."

If JD had tightened all the screws in his aircraft, this conversation might have awakened Harriet, but with the plane squeaking and rattling above the talk, she slept on.

"Now just take a look out your window," JD said; "what do you see down there?"

"Not much, but then I like space, scrub oaks, rolling prairie."

"That's great," JD said, "You know it's true what they say about taking the boy out of the country but not taking the country out of the boy."

"I go to yard sales off and on," Eddie said, "just to look for paintings of old farms and small creeks."

JD's hand-assembled aircraft roared past the eastern tip of Badlands National Park as he returned for a second to his old-swimming-hole philosophy.

"Every time I see those rocks poking out of the ground, I realize the 50s are as quiet as the Badlands. Big Icicle is as close as I'm ever going to get to *Happy Days*. And I just bored the hell out of you for 400 miles."

"Hey, don't worry, it's your plane; you pick the entertainment. I can tell you, nobody on this trip was bored for a minute."

156

But if JD had conceded the loss of the 50s, he hadn't lost his sense of incongruity. When the "modified" duct tape bandit bumped, bounced and fell down exhausted on a dirt strip of road outside Big Icicle, JD turned to Eddie and asked, "Want me to hail a cab for you?"

There's Always Beer

Chapter 37

The joke around Big Icicle was if anybody from out of state makes a second trip to the town, he's either lost or he's running from the in-laws. Hoping to have a little excitement in a place with only two kinds of coffee, hot and cold, JD spread the word that his Arizona friends would be staying another night at Motel 2. Thus, when he and the returnees arrived at Little Oak's place the evening before Zelda's memorial, the celebration—six friends, not counting the Graces—echoed up and down Icicle's main drag.

The local code of etiquette stipulated first, hug everybody for Zelda, second, break out Big I's Hair Thinner, and don't lose a lot of time between the two. The party-goers filled the biggest glasses they could find, made short appeals for world peace and safe bicycles and turned the rest over to chance.

As always, Eddie was caught unprepared when Little Oak asked him if he'd read any good myths lately; she was merely trying to steer the conversation away from Arizona politics and South Dakota weather. When Eddie didn't answer immediately, she helped him, "If you haven't inherited your folklore, you can always make some up; everybody does that anyway. A good myth ain't hard to find."

How in the world, Eddie asked himself, *does she know that*

I've been thinking about myths? Ah, it's just coincidence. Like the prototype doubter, the biblical Thomas, Eddie never seemed quite ready for certitude.

"JD here," Little Oak continued, "has a new myth every time you see him and then one by one they pass away, like weekends."

"Oh yeah," JD said, "well I got a real one this time. That low-flying plane thing is going to be big, and if you tell me there's a million bucks in my future, I'll take you up on the maiden flight."

One of the evening's guests said, "Let me know, JD, when your stock goes public. I got half a mill in antique phonebooks that's doing me no good."

Before the myth talk got further out of control, Little Oak said she had been thinking of leaving Motel 2. This quieted the locals momentarily. "I have never liked the idea of owning the land," she said. "It's against Native American tradition, myth, fable, whatever."

"But, you bought it and you have an official title," seemed to come simultaneously from each one in the group.

"Yes, the paperwork says it's mine," Little Oak said, "but that's not what tribal customs say."

"Ever think of Arizona?" Harriet asked, hopefully.

"You don't have to own the land to love it," Little Oak said. "Or maybe I just need to do something with my tepee. What do you think of re-upholstering the bishop's chair?"

"Sure you don't want to be an honorary co-pilot or steward-ess on the Transcontinental Arrow?" JD asked. "Tourists tip well. Tipping you know is another invented competition. Tippers are humiliated if they fail to live up to the ranking system that they themselves helped create."

Harriet raised the question that she had wanted to ask Little Oak since their first trip to Big Icicle, "How did you learn to read the future?"

Little Oak's answer was short, "The same way you learned to ride a bicycle. When you stopped falling over, you knew how to ride."

159

"No offence," Harriet said with disappointment in her voice, "we're in your house, but isn't that a little cavalier?"

"It is, but it's the best I have. Reading the future is an art, not a science, as they say."

JD took the side of a decades-old friend over that of Harriet the newcomer, "Whatever you call it, Little Oak's won-and-lost record is a fact."

When Eddie was about to chase his own theory of knowing things down another rabbit hole, Little Oak came back to Harriet's question about seers. She pointed again to her sign that read, "If you don't like my medicine, go to Walgreens." Then she thanked JD for his endorsement but insisted that mysteries and guesses have their places in forecasts. "In the end," she added, "the past is all we have; everything else is an experiment."

JD knew she was underselling herself and Eddie asked if she thought a lack of proof turns people toward myths, religions and superstitions.

"Yes," Little Oak said without hesitation, "because mysterious stories, by any other name, answer the big questions. They take some of the bumps out of the road."

"And then if you don't find the answers you're looking for," JD said, "there's always beer."

Harriet still wanted to know how Little Oak became so successful. Was it luck, fasting, self-discipline, sun gazing, auto suggestion, God's grace? If it was hard to believe that she had a hot line to the future, it was harder to believe that her successes were mere coincidence.

Little Oak said she couldn't answer Harriet's questions the way a farmer can tell you how many cattle are in his pasture. "The writer, for example, doesn't know where the muse comes from," she said. "If he did, he would call it in every morning before he sat down to work." She asked Eddie if he could tell them why he was fascinated with ducks. He wanted to try but not on an evening as special as this. "Maybe it's time to learn a lesson from apple trees," he said. "There's a process that puts apples on trees. It doesn't always make sense; it just makes apples."

Little Oak continued, "You're a long way from normal, my friends. In myths you are where life leaves the hard rules of point and counterpoint. Three years ago, I gave Harriet half of a short message and said the second half would come to her. I also said we would meet one more time. That has now happened. Oh, and don't wear your Sunday shoes tomorrow; there's a lot of new growth at the lake and the path is uneven in places."

Harriet was still curious, but in a spirit of fairness to all sides she thought, *Hey, I don't expect Father Ragone to clear up every question about the miracles in the Bible. So why should I now demand proof from Little Oak? It's quite enough that Eddie has spent his life wondering what's real. Hey, believe it or cut it loose.*

"Well, what's going to happen tomorrow for lunch?" JD asked. "I get hungry fast out in the country."

The chatter for the rest of the evening was light. Everybody enjoyed the pictures of the Graces' backyard before and after Zelda and no one missed the humor in South Dakota and Arizona as possible swing states in the next presidential election.

Then Harriet took the latest edition of the *Hearts Landing Monthly* that she had brought with her especially for that moment, opened it to the obituaries and held it up for the group. "See that," she said as she pointed to a picture of Zelda in a bright green frame. "When Zelda died," she said, "one of the two men in the maintenance truck that rainy day asked if it was alright to put something in the paper. The last line reads, 'That was the worst day that Rodney and I ever had on the job.'"

161

Little Things Matter

Chapter 38

At six the following morning, stillness had returned to Big Icicle, except for a couple of dogs and a foursome of women bikers. With Eddie, Harriet and JD in agreement, Little Oak parked her car farther from the lake than usual and they walked the rest of the way. They didn't want Zelda's memorial to seem like they were just driving up to mail a letter.

Re-thinking some of the complexities and hazards of remembrances, Harriet said, "You know, sometimes I think we come as much for the Reaper as the Reaper comes for us. We worry about a loss of dignity or propriety or reduced celestial impact if somewhere the services slip on a rule. All we really want today is to do the right thing for a dog."

Most of the funerals the Graces had attended for four decades were more rehearsed than random, more fixed than spontaneous. However, before they returned to the car that morning, they would be part of an ad hoc liturgy forever fixed in their memories.

Eddie followed Little Oak down the narrow trail that lead to the shoreline. After a hundred yards, JD, a little overweight for hiking, stopped to get his breath and Eddie waited for him. "Hey, Big Fella," JD said, "all that walking with Zelda turned you into a Daniel Boone. You must like it."

"I do," Eddie said, "I would walk with or without a dog."

Harriet and Little Oak went ahead.

"I'm glad to hear that because I've got an idea that might be the one we're looking for."

Remembering the flight from Sioux Falls, Eddie felt some shortness of breath himself.

"There are a lot of old people, older than us, who want to take walks but they're too scared to leave the house. Ever notice how slowly they go around corners; how they strap their shoes on a little tighter to get better support?"

Eddie thought, *And have you noticed that we need to have Zelda's memorial service sometime today?*

"I'll be brief. Old people want to get out but they worry about loose dogs. Their days of kicking big dogs in the chops are gone. Now they want protection."

Eddie thought, *Now this guy wants me to put these old people on a mile-long retractable rope and pull them back if they see a dog off a leash.*

"They need a scaled-down bodyguard–slim, trim and a good listener. That's you."

"They'd still be worried about big dogs," Eddie said.

"Right, but the odds of being bitten by a dog are what, ten thousand to one, and with you at their side, those odds double. These 80-year olds know that when two people are walking down the street and an aggressive dog comes charging at them there's a 50-50 chance that the mutt will bite the other guy."

"Now he wants me to take a bite for the old-timers."

"In a year," JD said, "we could open a place in Tucson. We could set up a web site–call it, Take The Bite Out Of Walking–maybe get some stimulus money."

By then, JD and Eddie had reached Ghost Dance where Little Oak checked the temperature of the water and Harriet checked out the canoe. Eddie still wasn't sure if a funeral was complete without candles and hymnals and some minor dignitary making an announcement of a future victory.

Little Oak carefully untied the canoe and brought it closer to a large rock to make it easier for Harriet to board. Since the boat had been built for no more than two small passengers, the question of who should accompany the ashes never arose. Matters of rank and ceremonial formats were not part of the thinking. The only rule was that Zelda's ashes should ride in the front.

As they were about to push off, JD handed Harriet the small paper bag that they had mistakenly assumed was the lunch he had talked about the night before. He said, "If you don't mind, I'd like you to leave this on the water after you've spread the ashes."

"What is it?" Harriet asked.

"It's a sandwich for Zelda. Call it, Peanut Butter and Love. The poor devil never got to finish the one she started at my house six years ago."

Eddie shuffled his feet nervously and said to JD, "I will see this picture forever."

JD said, "I had to do that. I don't make speeches like you do. Hell, I can't even make lunch that looks like lunch–raisins and sauerkraut–how would I ever do a eulogy?"

The two men moved to separate points along the shoreline while Little Oak and Harriet paddled the canoe slowly toward the lake's center.

"Will your husband give a talk for Zelda, today?" Little Oak asked. "I know he's a speech-maker."

"I don't think so," Harriet answered. "There was a time when he would have practiced a speech, rented a pavilion in a park and solemnized the occasion with a moment of silence. But none of that happened this time."

"There's great power in words," Little Oak said.

"And recently," Harriet said, "he's gotten more into symbols and speeches from the heart, although he pointed out just last week that if you're going to speak from your heart you'd better have your heart ready."

They stopped in the middle of the lake.

"Every evening around seven," Harriet said, "he celebrates a special moment from the day with a glass of wine and a toast. I laughed out loud the night he couldn't remember the day's highlight, so he raised his glass to that unknown person who made the very first batch of potato salad."

Little Oak laughed but continued to listen.

"But toasts aren't eulogies," Harriet said. "The night before we left, he said, 'Zelda will ride again on the front seat of the Volvo.' That short visual was as far as he could go with a tribute to Zelda. But there will be other times."

"He just needs practice with pictures," Sitting Bull's descendant said. "He'll soon become an expert."

"Change comes slowly for Eddie," Harriet said.

"Would it bother him if you and I offered Zelda a simple remembrance today without either a speech or much of an audience?" Little Oak asked.

"He will thank us for paying part of what he owes her," Harriet said.

"And do you think a story, a Zelda myth, is worth a dip in cold water?"

Harriet put her hand into the lake, "Tell me more."

"Can you swim a hundred yards today?"

"Yes, I certainly can."

"Then, if it's okay with you," Little Oak said looking in all directions to preserve the scene, "let's spread the ashes here, and then tow the canoe back to shore."

"Wow!" Harriet whispered, "I know the story. We'll have an empty canoe, like a riderless horse." Harriet always won the riddle-solving competitions.

"We will have a personal folktale," Little Oak said. "Each time we think of Zelda, we'll think of an empty canoe coming ashore. A small empty boat grips the soul the way a single eagle feather holds the spirit of the Oglala Sioux."

"Eddie will see it and immediately connect the symbol with John F. Kennedy's funeral procession," Harriet said. "Of course, we'll do it."

165

After Zelda's ashes and JD's sandwich had broken through the surface of the water, Little Oak hand-paddled the canoe a few yards away from the area. She and Harriet slid their bodies–feet first, face down–slowly over opposite sides of the canoe and into "memorial waters." The chill took the breath from Harriet like nothing had in a quarter century. "I must tell my philosopher husband that this water is no illusion; it's real."

Little Oak slipped the anchor rope loosely around Harriet's waist and asked, "Do you suppose the Queen of England has ever done something like this?"

"If she did," Harriet said, "she surely kept her hat on."

A slow backstroke allowed them to evaluate the short trip.

"An empty canoe in the water is an empty canoe in the water," Little Oak said, "but an empty canoe towed by a woman who just traveled 1,400 miles to spread the family dog's ashes on a cool, quiet lake in South Dakota? That can be a treasure–a replica of both joy and anguish."

"I'll remember the walks at dawn," Harriet said, "and Zelda's bobbing for ice cubes in July."

JD couldn't have felt more rewarded if he had found a multi-million-dollar investor in his sightseeing enterprise. Without taking his eyes off the lake, he re-joined Eddie.

"I wish I'd thought of the empty canoe image," Eddie said. "I came out here expecting to make a speech but all I needed was a picture–a picture of a canoe without a passenger. I will hold that speech a while. If you have more than one message on occasions like this, they tend to cancel each other out. The canoe is all we need."

"Hey Ed," JD said, "don't feel bad about not thinking of the empty canoe. Old pilot says if you have to fly some place, you don't have to fly the plane yourself; you just have to get there. And today a dog and an empty canoe and two women who know a lot about hearts just got you there."

That morning, Little Oak, Harriet, JD and Eddie walked away from Ghost Dance Lake very slowly. As they turned for a final look, three ducks swam out to the place where Zelda's ashes were left, to welcome their new neighbor.